CLOSING STAGES

A chilling case for Phyllida Moon

Phyllida Moon has to abandon any plans of a restful holiday with the love of her life in favour of an emergency operation. But Inspector Kendrick takes advantage of her need for convalescence to ask her to investigate some suspiciously premature deaths at Stansfield Manor Nursing Home. As usual, Phyllida's sleuthing involves acting a part – but this time she must act herself.

CLOSING STAGES

Eileen Dewhurst

Severn House Large Print
London & New York

This first large print edition published in Great Britain 2001 by
SEVERN HOUSE LARGE PRINT BOOKS LTD of
9-15, High Street, Sutton, Surrey, SM1 1DF.
First world regular print edition published 2000 by
Severn House Publishers, London and New York.
This first large print edition published in the USA 2002 by
SEVERN HOUSE PUBLISERS INC., of
595 Madison Avenue, New York, NY 10022

British Library Cataloguing in Publication Data

Dewhurst, Eileen
    Closing stages - Large print ed.
    1. Murder - Investigation - England
    2. Detective and mystery stories
    3. Large type books
    I. Title
    823.9'14 [F]

    ISBN 0-7278-7078-5

Printed and bound in Great Britain by
MPG Books Ltd, Bodmin, Cornwall.

One

After the funeral, the moment he was back inside, he went to his desk and brought out the photograph. He had told them he had destroyed it, because if he had not done so they would have destroyed it for him along with all the others, and that, in some strange way, would have been like losing his one piece of insurance.

So he would have to hide it away and bring it out only when he was alone in the house and the doors were locked. *Melodrama!* he thought, feeling his brief nervous smile, but he was as aware as they were of the danger. If it were ever to be seen it would bring everything crashing down.

Looking round the beloved and familiar room – anxiety and guilt mingling now with his painful sense of imminent separation – he wondered where would be the place to put the photograph, both for now and for after he had left. Somewhere easily accessible to him, but never to be discovered by other people. If he found the right place, he needn't worry if it ever came to a search of his home. Which of course it wouldn't, but for a brief hateful moment he saw the police riffling through his drawers, taking his pictures to pieces, prising up his new carpets ... Reluctantly he tried to put himself inside their minds as they pulled books from shelves, opened his work files and the files that held his personal interests.

Ah, that was it! The concealing of the pebble on the beach...

Work in the last few years had encroached on hobbies so relentlessly he hadn't touched the shabby old file for months, let alone added to it, and before he opened it he blew dust away. He couldn't even remember what he would find there, and he didn't reacquaint himself with any of the photographs already in the file; he merely rejoiced when he saw how many there were, and pushed the forbidden one in amongst them. The place was so safe, he could even leave it there when the removal men came to take everything away.

His immediate problem solved, he went back to his desk and took out the other photograph, the one they had told him he could keep. He took it to the window, and sat down in one of the armchairs turned to face the garden, trying not to look at the other which would always, now, be empty.

When he had studied the photograph for a while he turned his sorrowful gaze on to the familiar view. It was a quiet evening, appropriately weatherless, he thought, for this time of loss – the sister, and then, so soon afterwards, the brother – low grey sky without feature and the branches of the trees unmoving. She'd sat there with him, his lovely clever Peggy who smiled at him now only out of a photograph, before and during her dreadful descent. There was one particular flowering tree by the downward slope of the garden which always reminded him of the terrible moment he had received proof incontrovertible that his fears were justified, because he had been looking at it as Peggy spoke...

But the fears had, of course, begun a long time before that. The spring day at their favourite lunch place, perhaps, when it had been so mild they'd eaten in the garden and he hadn't been able to make her aware of the bird song. And then the next time they'd gone there in the rain and had their lunch indoors...

7

Not wanting to, for a moment fighting against it, he was unable to hold back from recalling the relentless process that had brought him to this moment and the enormous divide he was about to cross.

Two

In the event, Phyllida never took up the Edinburgh hotel booking she had made following her oh-so-uncharacteristic decision to give herself at least one more sight of the only man she had ever met who she believed could become the love of her life.

As herself, she had seen him only once. During the other, earlier, meetings, she had been the wry-humoured, red-haired Scottish woman she always found the hardest to play because she was the nearest of her cast of characters to herself. Perhaps that was what had given her that unfamiliar courage, which had shocked and dismayed her even as she made her plans to pursue Dr Pusey to Scotland: her knowledge that the large cheerful man with sorrow lurking at the back of his eyes had been attracted to someone so like Phyllida Moon. Having to turn away from him, to lie to him that she was married to a non-existent beloved husband,

9

had been the hardest act of her life, let alone of her career as an actress turned private eye who sleuthed in character.

She had met him as herself when the charade, and the investigation for which it had been devised, were over. She had driven a few miles inland from Seaminster to the small Botanic Gardens of which he was Director, and after walking and sitting a while in the sun she had gone to the cafe and found him alone there, tackling a large late lunch. There was a captioned photograph of him on the wall which had enabled her, when she had eaten her sandwich, drunk her coffee, and exchanged a couple of polite smiles, to pause by his table on her way out and thank him for the Gardens which, she had lied, she always so much enjoyed visiting. The politeness had continued for a few seconds, and then she had seen in the kind eyes a reminder of what as the red-haired Scot she had seen there.

It had been enough for that time, and anyway she had been reluctantly on her way to London to take a leading role in a new television crime series. The reluctance was part native disinclination to be in the spotlight (the spotlight that would fall on Phyllida Moon when she was not on the set), and partly the twin fears of losing the

10

anonymity which was the crucial basis for her detective work, and of risking her eponymous boss, Peter Piper, discovering he could carry out the work of his Agency perfectly well without her. This last fear, Phyllida had soon realised, was the chief reason for her reluctance: the TV contract was a thrilling adventure, but her work at the south coast detective agency was the staple occupation of her days (and sometimes nights), and the last thing she could ever bear to lose.

Unless a miracle took place in Scotland...

When the shooting of *A Policeman's Lot* was over and she was back in Seaminster, Phyllida had gone a second time to the Gardens and learned that its Director had left to take up a senior position at the Royal Botanic Garden in Edinburgh. She had dragged herself out of her angry disappointment – successfully, she had thought, but that could have been because she hadn't quite been able to accept his departure as the end: when Peter had suggested she take a holiday following her last dangerous and exhausting investigation, she had booked a week in Scotland's capital city.

And then, in the small hours of a night shortly before her holiday was to begin, Phyllida had been wakened by a pain at her centre so agonising that after a short struggle she had reached for her bedside telephone and rung the local hospital. So that when she should have been turning her car northwards she was drowsing in a hospital bed minus her gall bladder.

"You look terrible," Peter greeted her cheerfully on his first visit.

"Do I? Well, I don't feel terrible any more, but then I couldn't have gone on feeling the way I did, and live."

"I'm so sorry, Phyllida." Peter tossed back the ever-falling flop of blond hair from his forehead, the brown eyes in his thin brown face shining with feeling as sincere as Phyllida had ever seen in them. And she had no grounds in experience for her instinct that Peter, as kind as he was clever, lacked the capacity for deep emotion.

"It was never life-threatening."

"Thank heaven. What about your holiday?"

"Cancelled from my sick bed."

"That's a shame. You know..." The expressive face was full of anxiety as it studied hers.

"What?"

"You look dreadfully delicate. I think you should go to a nursing home for a week or so, really take it easy."

"Oh no!" Her face didn't change, but he saw in her eyes the unwelcome shock he had given her. He didn't know, of course (and, when he thought about it, he didn't want to know), but an instinct from the start of their working relationship had told him that here was a woman capable of profound though controlled feeling – to the extent that sometimes, to his vague discomfort, he felt himself to be superficial by comparison. (And he did seem, so far in his life, to have got over his numerous emotional setbacks fairly easily.) "That's quite unnecessary, Peter!"

"Well, then ... Go away somewhere, if not to Scotland. I mean, it's not as if Edinburgh's sacrosanct, is it?"

"Of course not." She hadn't told him – or anyone else – why it had been her holiday choice. "If you like I'll have a couple of lazy days at home, but the best thing for me then will be to get back to work."

"Um. Well, we'll talk about it on my next visit." Her forehead was glistening and she looked fearfully tired. But as soon as he had got to his feet, Peter sat abruptly down again. "I must just tell you ... I was going to tell you the minute I arrived but you threw me, looking so frail." They grinned at one another, each vaguely rejoicing in the strength of their sibling-like relationship.

13

"Kendrick rang. To ask if he could speak to Miss Bowden. Now, there's a first!"

Detective Chief Superintendent Kendrick of Seaminster Constabulary had found himself on a number of occasions, without requesting it and very grudgingly, accepting the assistance of the Peter Piper Detective Agency in the person of its Miss Bowden. (Miss Bowden, of course, was Phyllida, investigating in disguise on behalf of an Agency client a disquieting situation that had ultimately exploded into murder or some other mayhem serious enough to bring the police in.) Kendrick had even begun to find himself, when deciding to visit the scene of a violent crime (the DCS was a hands-on chief beyond the taste of several of his senior officers) cowering mentally before the prospect of Miss Bowden awaiting him *in situ*, in possession of otherwise unattainable information he would be forced to sue for.

Despite Dr Piper's assurances, Kendrick had never been able to bring himself to quite believe that Miss Bowden was the Agency's only female field operative. He had interviewed her in a number of guises ranging from daily woman to husky-voiced American sophisticate, without ever, he was frustratedly aware, encountering the woman

14

herself. Aware in her turn of the Chief Superintendent's reluctant obsession with her identity, Phyllida sometimes wondered how he would react if he were to discover that Miss Bowden herself was a work of fiction.

Phyllida Moon, it had been decided at the start of her work for the Agency, would appear under her own name solely on the Agency's books, and nowhere as her undisguised self. Miss Bowden had been invented by Peter and Phyllida during a hasty conversation on their mobiles the first time a confrontation had suddenly loomed between a disguised Miss Moon and the local constabulary. In due course the unadorned Mary Bowden – a no-nonsense, unglamorous woman with a tight French pleat, ten years or so older than Phyllida's thirty-five, the sort of woman people would not be quite sure they had met before – had become her office persona. She enabled Phyllida, instead of slipping out of sight when a client or would-be client came into the Agency, to stand her ground and recently, at Peter's suggestion, take on the occasional straightforward case as her own.

"What on earth did he want?"

"He didn't say. When I told him Miss Bowden was in Seaminster Hospital losing her gall bladder he said he'd come back to us."

"You told him she was here?"

"Well, yes..." The anxiety in his eyes was more fleeting than the anxiety in hers. "He's hardly likely to come looking for you. And even if he did, you aren't the least bit like Miss Bowden, let alone any of your other characters."

"Thanks for the reassurance about Miss Bowden."

"My pleasure, and the truth. So you mustn't get paranoid about your identity, my girl. Kendrick's never heard of Phyllida Moon."

"I know. It's just that I've started having the odd nightmare about being recognised after *A Policeman's Lot* comes to TV screens in the autumn."

"You won't be. And even if you are, your real name won't be in the credits – and thanks to Mary Bowden, PM will continue to be unconnectable to the Agency. In the worst case scenario, you'll always be a layer away from discovery."

"I know," she said again. "It's just that my work with the Agency's so important to me."

"To me, too. I'm a lucky chap. Far luckier than I deserve." Peter got to his feet again,

16

dropped a kiss on her cheek, and was turning away as a nurse appeared carrying a small vase containing the freesias he had brought her.

"Intimate flowers are the best in hospital." Phyllida held them to her face before setting them down on her locker. "Thank you, Peter."

"I'll be in again tomorrow."

"I'll look forward. Put your head round the day room door first when you arrive; I'm hoping to be there by the morning."

It seemed incredible to go so quickly from agony to convalescence, but that was what she was doing. Phyllida had her best night's sleep for weeks, and by coffee time the next morning had taken possession of a comfortable long chair in the day room, in front of a window that flooded light on to her book. She was determined to take a rest from attempts to answer her own permanently hovering question – had her sudden illness saved her from a foolish and possibly painful journey, or was it merely making her postpone an action it was pivotal in her life that she should undertake? She was almost confident the fat nineteenth-century novel on her lap would ensure that she stuck to her intention for an hour or two at least.

She had the day room to herself and

peace, regained bodily comfort and the good light enabled her to go deep into Mrs Gaskell's absorbent pages. It was several seconds after the sound of the door opening that she looked up and saw the tall man standing just inside the room and gazing intently at the only person in it.

All his eyes were doing was questioning her; there was no recognition in them. She could have smiled politely, returned her own eyes to her book, and he would have gone away. But the shock was so great Phyllida reacted to it involuntarily, hearing her gasp of breath, feeling the surprise leap into her eyes, and finding her hand suddenly and protectively at her breast.

She undid all these things in a flash, but it was too late. He was crossing the room towards her, sitting down on the chair beside hers, looking into her face, now, with confidence.

But without a trace of the triumph she would have expected. And when he at last spoke his usually crisp voice was gentle.

"Miss Bowden?"

She had to nod, of course. There was no alternative.

"I didn't come to flush you out," Kendrick said, easing back slightly in the chair that was creaking under his long bulk. "I came to see one of my men who was injured a couple of nights ago trying to break up a fight. But Dr Piper told me yesterday that his Miss Bowden was in this hospital recovering from an operation and I couldn't resist looking in here as I went past..."

"So it seems that it had to be, Chief Superintendent!" Phyllida spoke in her most extravagant stage mode, striking her breast this time with intent. It must be the anaesthetic, or the trauma of major surgery, that was making her take this alarming event so insouciantly, and so very much out of her own character.

Kendrick laughed, and she saw the relief in his eyes. Surprise, too. But she had surprised herself as well.

"Another disguise?" he asked her.

"I'm not at work, Mr Kendrick," she answered him. "I could go into *this* kind of theatre only as myself." It was a confession she had made a number of times alone, waking and sleeping, always in a surround of the utmost dread. Yet here she was, now she had really made it, almost enjoying the experience. "You've had the devil's own luck, haven't you?"

"I have," he said humbly. "And it's making me feel guilty. Especially as I'm going to ask one other—"

"Coffee, Miss Moon? The usual? Dash of milk, no sugar?"

Busty, bustling little probationer Tracy had steered her trolley across the room with her usual bravura, and was standing expectantly in front of them, coffee pot in hand.

"Thank you, Tracy. Could my visitor have a cup, too? If he'd like one?"

Phyllida had turned swiftly to Kendrick as Tracy spoke, not giving him time to banish the look of one who has already had a drink. Of cream.

"Thanks. Black, please. Two sugars."

The silence between them continued for a few seconds after Tracy had left, broken only by the tinkle of a couple of coffee spoons in contact with pottery.

"Luckier," Phyllida said at last, softly, "than I would have thought possible."

"Would you have told me?"

"I don't know. You were starting to ask me, weren't you?"

"Yes. Because I wanted to know for myself." Kendrick brought the sentence out on a confessional rush. And it seemed only fair.

"Just as you want to know whether Miss Bowden really is only one woman." She was behaving as if she was alone and conjuring up yet another scenario of exposure. Yet she knew that a real man was there beside her, and was still not afraid. "Peter told you she was, but I'm not sure you believed him. He was telling you the truth, though, Chief Superintendent. Do you believe *me*?"

"Yes." For that moment at least, looking into the steady grey-green eyes, he did believe her. With difficulty – her achievement was so unlikely ... Kendrick realised he would have been happier if she had confessed to being less than the sum of the women he had met through her. "But you have an extraordinary talent."

"I'm a good actress. I've been one all my adult life. That's all."

"I doubt it. You'll tell me your whole name, now?"

"Phyllida Moon. The only place I appear in the Agency set-up is its books. Miss Bowden in one form or another is my public face."

"How do you cope in the course of your job with men – people – who want to give you a lift home? See you again?" Kendrick tried to banish his annoyance at thinking of the husky-voiced American sophisticate he had reluctantly found so attractive.

"I've gone so far now, I'll tell you." He had settled his length back into his chair and his eyes were bright with simple but intense

21

curiosity, almost convincing Phyllida that his questions were on behalf of his own peace of mind. She closed her book and leaned back herself so that their faces were on a level. They were close enough for her to see reflected in those dark, deep-set eyes her own surprise at the sudden amicable proximity between herself and the man whom until this moment she had seen as her adversary. There was a moment when she wondered if she should be seeking Peter's authority, but it passed as she realised it had never been he who had insisted on Phyllida Moon's anonymity. "Phyllida Moon has a permanent booking at the Golden Lion, across Dawlish Square from the Agency office. A back bedroom that I think of as my workplace. Peter was helpful once to the management there, and apparently the manager never felt he could adequately repay him. He and his staff know the set-up, field phone calls and visits. To anyone I get to know on the job, my character's staying at the Golden Lion – I get collected from there and taken back there. And I always go home from there as myself." As Phyllida paused for further mental editing of her work situation she saw Kendrick bite his nether lip and suspected he was forbidding himself another question which would appear greedy and which, anyway, he knew she wouldn't answer, that day at least. "That's my ultimate disguise, you see, Chief Superintendent. Mine own self."

It had to be the anaesthetic: she felt as if she had been drinking. She was putting on a performance in her own persona – which, she suddenly realised, was unprecedented: it was only in disguise, hitherto, that she had ever gone even slightly over the top. Phyllida was shaken to find herself having to make an effort not to tell Kendrick about her fears for the autumn, when, whatever Peter said to reassure her, there would be a danger of that precious anonymity being lost. But that would mean telling him about *A Policeman's Lot*, which was so far unnecessary. Just as it was unnecessary to tell him about the book she was writing on the history of women and the stage...

"So there you have it, Mr Kendrick." Phyllida sat upright as she struggled to regain her usual alertness to danger. "I hope you won't feel insulted when I ask you, please, to keep the information I've just given you strictly to yourself. I can't think you would pass it on to anyone, but I have to ask you."

"Of course you do, Mrs Moon." Kendrick matched her slight return to attention, so that their faces were still level. His mind was a whirl of triumph and astonishment, with the old annoyance creeping back that he should be taking the question of Dr Piper's female field staff so seriously and personally. "And of course I shall keep your secret." From everyone but Miriam; if he didn't tell the wife who had come back to him, he would know that he really was giving too much importance to this drably elegant woman who had turned out to be the pearl in Piper's enigmatic oyster ... Good grief, Kendrick thought irritably, she was even subverting the usual spareness of his thought processes.

"*Miss* Moon, actually. When I left my husband I reverted to my maiden name. A-h-h! Excuse me a moment. I'm getting stiff and I must move."

Phyllida wavered to her feet and Kendrick, guilty again, watched her take a few uncertain steps backwards and forwards in front of their chairs, Phyllida wondering as she walked if she was making them slightly more tentative than they need be. She was in a housecoat and she wasn't quite upright, but even so the Chief Superintendent found it easier to recall the tall elegance of the American than the bent bustle of the daily woman or even the prim, jerky movements of the meagre Miss Bowden. Yet the overall effect of Miss Moon was so muted he had to study her sallow, bruised-eyed face to discover how good its features were.

"That's better." Phyllida sat carefully down. "But I must go for a real walk in a moment."

"And I must leave you. I'm sorry, your story's made me forget you're not well. And why I wanted to see Miss Bowden. Could you spare me another few—"

"Peter told me when he came in yesterday that you'd rung the Agency and asked for Miss Bowden. Of course. Tell me what you wanted."

"Thank you."

Although Phyllida had been talking about her work at the Peter Piper Agency, their conversation had somehow not been about business. Now all at once it was and both of them straightened up, moving to the edge of their chairs.

"I wanted to ask you if you would undertake an unofficial investigation. At Stansfield Manor nursing home. D'you know it?"

"I know of it." Alarm bells were at last ringing. "That it's fairly new but has been going long enough to have acquired a good reputation. There's no way, though, Chief Superintendent, that I could maintain a disguise in such intimate—"

"I realise that. I wasn't going to ask you to go in as a patient. But now..." Kendrick tried to see her objectively and decided, on a brief pang of conscience, that she really did look ill. But the unhappy coincidence was too convenient to let go, and the professional in him made him press on. "You're obviously not well enough to consider going back to work right away, or even going home and looking after yourself." He realised as he spoke that his assumption she was currently without a partner might offend her, but her expressionlessly attentive face didn't change. "You'll benefit from a week or two in a nursing home, and you'll be helping me. Stansfield Manor, as you say, is one of the area's better ones. You would be doing me a very great favour" – to have said that, once, would have put him in danger of choking – "and your fees would be paid. You'd go in as yourself," he went on quickly, as her face clouded and she raised a hand. "All I would ask is for you to keep your eyes and ears open. And if you see or hear anything disquieting, I would like you to go in as a careworker when you're completely recovered."

"Anything disquieting?" Mingling with

26

her own disquiet, now, was the familiar surge of adrenalin.

Kendrick felt what Phyllida saw: a quick surge of colour into and out of his strong-featured face. "It sounds absurd, I know, but a cousin of my wife's was in there recently for a few weeks, and became friendly with a woman who died. The place takes those who need to convalesce or want a last home, but a resident who becomes the victim of Alzheimer's or senile dementia will be allowed to remain if they don't make excessive demands on the staff, and patients already in the early stages of mental illness are sometimes accepted. This woman was on the way over the mental edge, but she appeared physically fit. My wife's cousin is a nurse, and she was very surprised when the death occurred: the woman had had a mild chest infection which the doctor had diagnosed as such, but there hadn't appeared to be any cause for alarm. Mary didn't see the woman after she'd said goodnight to her one bedtime, and when she queried her absence at coffee time the following morning she was told she'd had a heart attack during the night that had carried her off." Kendrick paused and cleared his throat. "She told me that years working as a nurse makes you sense when your patient's near a natural end. This woman was only an acquaintance, of course, but Mary said there was nothing about her that suggested imminent demise."

"Did she ask any questions?"

"Scarcely. She just expressed her surprise, and the director and the senior sister agreed they'd been surprised, too."

"Um. Had any relatives been in to see the dead woman the day before?"

"That was Mary's first thought. But the woman appeared to be alone in the world. Just a distant nephew who never came near but who, Mary learned through gossip, is apparently sole heir to a small nest egg. As I said, she'd seen the doctor a few days earlier because of the chest infection, so he was able to sign the death certificate. Heart failure."

"Quite honestly, Chief Superintendent, it doesn't sound very worrying."

"Not on the surface, no. And before you remind me, I know anyone, at any age, and however healthy, can die suddenly. But I'm acting unofficially – at this stage – and, I hope, with unofficial resources." It was the first time Phyllida had seen Maurice Kendrick smile, and she was surprised by the charm of it. "And there *is* one other factor."

"Yes?" The adrenalin was making her feel

dramatically less feeble.

"There was a bit of a kerfuffle going on the day Mary went in. When she asked a nurse that evening what had been happening she was told a resident had unexpectedly died. Of heart failure. The nurse had gone on to say, a bit shamefacedly, that perhaps it was a blessing all round, as the poor lady was starting to get very confused."

Kendrick broke off and resumed the intent expression Phyllida had first seen in his face.

"How long between the two deaths?"

"A couple of weeks." Kendrick was silent for a moment, then leaned very slightly towards her. "You'll need a recovery period, you know."

"I expect you're right," Phyllida responded slowly. "If Peter thinks so, too, you can book me into Stansfield Manor, Chief Superintendent."

Three

So when did it start?

A question, of course, I realise on reflection that I cannot answer. I can only try to recall the first time I noticed that something might be wrong.

Try?

It's the last effort I want to make.

But since I left the old world and entered the new, I find the coldness of my new life forcing me to rake through the warm ashes of my memories.

To write the biography of her last years.

I must be careful, or it will be as dangerous as the photograph. I know it would be safer – and less anguishing – to write nothing at all. But I find I am unable to let her go so easily.

Perhaps it was the charming absent-mindedness that had always been part of her that made me so slow to understand. Even made me, I am being forced to confess, irritable before I was alarmed.

Yes, I've recalled the first time she made me wonder. We were sitting by the window on a summer evening after dinner. I remember the patio doors were slightly open and the sun was going down in a welter of spreading gore. Peggy had the latest "literary" novel open on her lap, and whenever I looked up for the assurance of her presence she appeared to be reading.

But when my head was down over my newspaper she said, "It's bleeding."

"What is, darling?" I spoke without looking up, and it was the silence following my question that made me raise my head.

"Darling?" She was staring out through the window, and every part of her was trembling. "What is it?" I remember I took her hand, and that it went inert in mine. "What's bleeding?"

"The sky. All over. Look. When it's bled dry, what shall we do? What will poor robin do then, poor thing?"

A nursery rhyme. I remembered her reciting it to our daughter Susie when she was a little girl, and for a moment I persuaded myself she was teasing me. But then I looked into her eyes and I saw that she was truly afraid.

"Darling ... Don't be frightened. There's nothing—"

The trembling ceased.

"Goodness, Eric, you're looking so solemn! Whatever is the matter?"

Her eyes now were laughing in their customary joyous way. I remember wondering, hopefully, if I had been the one to have an aberration.

"I just thought..." To my shame now, I found myself testing her. "That sky is almost too much ... Too big and red?"

"Eric! It's beautiful! You are the most awful philistine. D'you have to see everything in terms of the human body in imperfect condition?"

"No, of course not. Come here..."

Her brother Robert – tacitly acknowledged by the Family as their Golden Boy – walked in as we were embracing. He'd looked after our house for a couple of weeks earlier in the year when we'd been away, and he hadn't returned the key. I'd no family left of my own when Peggy became my wife, and we'd been married only a short time before I found myself feeling her family considered themselves to be mine, too, in more than law, that they'd "taken me on". So I hadn't been surprised about the key, and wasn't surprised then when Robert suddenly appeared. That was how they were.

Even now I'm not sure Peggy's reaction to the sunset was really the start of it. Except perhaps as a brief, horrified precognition on her part that made her see that sky as a metaphor for what was to become of her.

After that it was much less dramatic. Simply, at first, an intermittent loss of memory which, it hurts me now to recall, I met with exasperation. And surprise. I had always believed Peggy to be as clever as the rest of her clan, even though she hadn't harnessed her brain to a profession as the others – apart from Freddie – had done.

She herself was annoyed by her early lapses. I can see her now, calling me to sit down beside her on the sofa while she confessed to having forgotten to do some small thing I'd asked of her. Getting bread, or potatoes, for God's sake. Poor Peggy! In the early days she used to laugh at herself, but after a while I saw glimpses of the fear the red sky had brought her. At least, at that stage, our eyes met and mutually understood as they had always done.

Until one day, I suppose three or four months after the forgetfulness began, when I came into the sitting room and found her fiddling with the blind cord.

"What is it?" I crossed the room and stood beside her for a few moments, just watching her restless fingers. "What's wrong with it?"

"Can't you see?" She turned to me, and it was the worst moment of my life. Her face was distorted with anxiety, her eyes its desperate focus. They raked mine for reassurance, but without acknowledgement that I was anything but a window through which help must come. The complicity had left them, the awareness that I was me.

I must leave it there for the time being, it hurts so much. In any case, I'm a busy man with a great deal to do, and duty calls.

Four

"D'you like your room, Mrs Moon?"

"It's lovely!" Phyllida made no attempt to correct the sobriquet: she and Peter had decided that even in the third millennium a married woman would be less likely than a single to be questioned on what she did for a living.

The moment they entered the room the young careworker had taken her across its considerable width to the deep bay window, where they were now standing looking out over a long downward slope of lawn bounded by broad curving beds of herbaceous plants at their high summer peak, which were backed in their turn by old sandstone walls partly hidden by a rich variety of climbing plants. At its foot the garden seemed to melt into the pattern of small fields beyond it, a gently undulating patchwork defined by the darker green of its dividing hedges.

"You don't see that kind of countryside so much nowadays," Phyllida lamented.

"Don't you? It's fab, isn't it? And this room has the best view." Careworker Debbie, flushed with what Phyllida read as a proprietorial pride in the amenities she was presenting, turned to face her.

"I can believe it." She hadn't expected accommodation as modest as her permanent space at the Golden Lion, but she had hardly foreseen this luxury. Could it be the Detective Chief Superintendent's way of thanking her for having come so very clean, to the extent of completely letting him off the hook of his obsession with the size of Dr Piper's female workforce? Whatever it was, he had ensured she would at least enjoy the background to her activities at Stansfield Manor.

"It's more like a hotel room than a room in a nursing home." More to her taste than a hotel room, in fact. The non-institutional furniture lacked the usual grand hotel curlicues, the decor – white walls, pale gold curtains – lacked the hectic patterning associated with hotel decor, and the room's proportions would have been impeccable if one corner hadn't disappeared behind a small half-open door through which Phyllida glimpsed bathroom fitments. Not, this time, to her surprise: Maurice Kendrick had assured her she would have the opportunity to make her own ablutions.

"It was one of the main bedrooms when the Manor was a private house. You can read about it, there are leaflets at Reception ... This booklet tells you how the TV works, and your bathroom's through that door. How much help d'you need?"

"None. This couple of weeks is pure self-indulgence."

"Is it?" The bright swooping glance lingered for a critical moment on Phyllida's face. "You don't look so well. Anyway, just ring if there turns out to be anything. You can have your meals up here, you know, if you'd like. Or come down to the dining room, of course."

"Oh, I'll come down to the dining room." Kendrick hadn't needed to ask her to eat in public; the adrenalin would demand it.

"Great. You'll have to have breakfast in bed, though, I'm afraid. Everyone does. It's just cereal, toast or rolls and tea or coffee, but the other meals make up for it."

"That I can believe. And toast and tea's all I ever have."

"That's all right, then."

Debbie, having obviously taken to Mrs Moon – Phyllida acknowledged it with a modest reluctance she would not have felt had Debbie taken to one of her characters –

twirled her puppy-plump body on one contrastingly slim leg, but made no move towards the door. So Phyllida sat down on the edge of the bed and asked her if she was happy working at the Manor.

"I should say! It's not easy to get in here, you know. You have to have your NVQ, of course – that's the National Vocational Qualification – or be working towards it, but that doesn't automatically get you in, even if there's a vacancy."

"That's interesting, Debbie. But how do you know?"

"The friend who suggested I try for a job here was turned down. She had all her certificates so she felt brave enough to ask why. They told her 'a certain maturity' was required." So perhaps Kendrick hadn't been as fanciful as she had thought him, suggesting she return as a careworker. "I wouldn't have put that down as one of my qualifications, so I was gobsmacked when I was taken on."

"Well done! You say 'they' had turned your friend down? And I presume interviewed you?"

"Oh, yeah; the Director had the Senior Sister sitting in on the interview, and one of the Manor's two doctors. It scared me shi – it really scared me, I can tell you. Not that

38

they were anything but kind, they talked quietly and didn't bully me at all, it was just that they were so *serious*, and I did feel out-numbered." Debbie giggled. "The Lord only knows how I made it."

"Well, you did. What hours d'you work?"

"Five days a week. And a day's a day here, I can tell you, Mrs Moon. Eight till eight, with half an hour for lunch."

"So careworkers tend to leave?"

"No! Well, some do, of course, usually the youngest and the boys. They don't have us girls' staying power. But more of the women stay than go. It's a good job."

"Not like working with mentally sick people."

So as not to crowd the girl Phyllida made it a statement rather than a question, getting to her feet as she spoke and going across the room to open the suitcase Debbie had placed on the appropriate rack.

"Well..." Out of the corner of her eye Phyllida saw Debbie twirl again. "There *are* a few; the Manor sometimes takes people in the early stages of mental illness. And some have got that way since coming in and are allowed to stay."

"Until they die?"

"One or two people have died since I came to work here, but they hadn't been – like that – for very long and they weren't all that far gone, so I don't really know." Phyllida had turned to look at Debbie, who was standing, hand on hip, unfazed. "I suppose it depends how bad people get. Nobody's been sent away since I started working here."

"I see." That if any murderous activity had taken place at Stansfield Manor, it looked as though Debbie had had no part in it. "So you're qualified in EMI work?" The Chief Superintendent had suggested Phyllida start acquiring knowledge of the role he hoped she would play later, and the first thing she had learned was that homes for the Elderly Mentally Ill were in a category of their own.

"Only the very junior careworkers are taken on without EMI qualifications. The Manor isn't registered as an EMI home, but the Director told me in my interview that the borderline between sanity and insanity can be very thin."

In the last minute or so Debbie had twice glanced towards the door. It was time, for now, to stop asking questions. Phyllida strolled over to her. "I've kept you long enough, you polite and patient girl. So what time should I present myself for lunch?"

"One o'clock. I'll just turn the telly on for you, shall I?"

"Oh ... Yes. Thanks."

Phyllida waited until Debbie's sturdy footfalls had faded along the wide corridor beyond her door before turning it off, then grabbed the notebook that lived in her bag and wrote down one thing the girl had said – *They hadn't been like that very long and they weren't all that far gone* – before going over to the window to watch the two people who had emerged on to the lawn and were circling it in earnest conversation.

One was the Director of the home, to whom John Bright, the owner of the Golden Lion Hotel, had introduced her before taking his leave. The Chief Superintendent had not needed to suggest that it would be inadvisable in the circumstances for Phyllida to be introduced to Stansfield Manor by either a policeman or a local private investigator, and she and Peter had had a rather depressing few moments realising how difficult it was going to be to find anyone at all untainted by the shadow, at least, of the Law. In the end Peter had turned to John Bright, who had already shown his respect for the privacy of a private eye by asking no questions at all about Phyllida's permanent need of one of his back bedrooms. True to form, he had accepted Peter's tentative invitation with no

41

questions about why Miss Moon's work connections were to be kept secret, even offering to claim temporary kinship with her when he booked her in. Peter and Phyllida had gratefully accepted the offer, and so Phyllida had entered the office of Dr Charles Hartley, Director of Stansfield Manor, as the cousin of the manager of the Golden Lion Hotel.

Dr Hartley was a neat, slight man with a light voice and shiny dark hair, whose small spectacles were somehow a prominent feature of his appearance. A shy man, Phyllida had thought, a little awkward in conversation. Unlike the other man who had been in the Director's office when she and John had been taken there on their arrival.

The Director had introduced him as Dr Jonathan Clifford, and told them that he was one of the two local GPs who looked after those patients who did not express a wish to retain the services of the doctor with whom they had been registered before entering the Manor.

"That makes me a busy man for my pains," Dr Clifford had said ruefully, as Phyllida approved his easy manner and his appearance: tall, classically good-looking, with a straight blue-eyed gaze and hair as fair as Peter's. "The Manor has a good reputation, Mrs Moon, Mr Bright" – but he was looking only at Phyllida – "and I can make the boast, you see, not being a part of the establishment. People tend to come from quite far away, beyond their former GP's area – though I can't complain too much, with there being another general practitioner to share the job with me. Can you believe it, some of the patients actually seem to prefer her ministrations to mine?"

Dr Clifford's agreeably disconcerting gaze was softened by a teasing smile as he turned it on the Director, who made an economical gesture of demur with small, well-manicured hands before thanking him, with a tight little smile of his own, for the plug. Despite the formality of Dr Hartley's response, Phyllida had gained the impression that he was at home with this delectable GP and his relaxed manner – and now here they were in the garden, the younger and taller man with his arm thrown across the Director's shoulder as they began another circuit.

She had not been so sure of the Director's relations with the Senior Sister, who had come into the office as John Bright was leaving and announced her job title in a tone that gave Phyllida a mental picture of

43

the two capital letters. She was a tall, severe-faced woman silently proclaiming her competence, in almost ludicrous contrast to the small-scale Director with his anxious manner and smudge of moustache, who reminded Phyllida irresistibly of Captain Mainwaring of *Dad's Army*. A couple of tartars, perhaps, perpetually vying for top spot? Which would have to mean a clash of personalities rather than a scrambling for position in the hierarchy – their roles were clearly complementary, and both names appeared in the Manor's brochure as heading their respective fields. Sister Caroline had the physical advantage with her height and proud carriage, and a pleasing, low-pitched voice which Phyllida had been pleasantly surprised to hear after taking in the determined features and potentially aggressive stance. But with so positive an appearance – she was a good-looking woman of the type that tends to be called handsome – she probably found it more impressive to suggest resources as yet unused. Phyllida knew well from her years on stage that to portray a weak character, not always in control, she must put her from the start on top doh to show that she has little or nothing in reserve.

Somewhere beyond her door a deep-toned

clock struck the half-hour. Descent to lunch was imminent. Adrenalin surging, Phyllida turned from the window to unpack her suitcase at least as far as the things that were liable to crush. It seemed strange, she reflected as she moved about the room, to be on the job as herself, unpacking her own clothes and putting so little make-up on the glass shelf in the bathroom. In place of the array in the bathroom at the Golden Lion she could here muster only a pot of moisturiser, a bottle of light foundation and a couple of pale lipsticks. Strange, too, to be tidying her own short cap of hair and seeing her own slightly wary expression in the mirror over the washbowl. Always, when she was assuming a character, she thought and moved according to her perception of that person as she put on her clothes, so that by the time she sat down at her dressing-table for wig and make-up her mouth and eyes, her whole expression, were already transformed. Now it was just sallow-skinned, straight-eyed Phyllida Moon returning her critical gaze. And suddenly, as she realised she was enjoying the unique experience of sleuthing as herself, her mouth widened and the solemn eyes lit up in a smile.

A smile that Jack Pusey would one day see? And if he did see it, would it affect him the way it had affected him when he had seen it on the face of the character she was least unlike?

The smile became a frown as Phyllida reproved herself for self-indulgence. She might not be in character but she *was* at work, and the Phyllida Moon who was investigating a couple of deaths at Stansfield Manor at the personal invitation of Seaminster's third most senior policeman was not the woman who had run about the remote edges of the Botanic Gardens crying aloud when she had learned that Dr Pusey had gone to Edinburgh.

Anyway, her illness appeared to have exaggerated her negative characteristics – her sallowness, her thinness, her misleading impression of fragility – and it was even more unlikely than usual that any man, let alone the man she could love, would look at her twice.

Reimposing the smile in rueful mode, Phyllida made the quick but comprehensive sweep of bathroom and bedroom for listening devices which was essential Agency practice in respect of all premises occupied during an ongoing investigation. As she had expected it proved negative, but nothing in the business could be taken for granted. She slung her bag over her shoulder with a sigh of relief before standing to attention a moment to impose the sense of dedication that came without bidding when she was in disguise. Then she took hold of the flowered enamel door handle, pulled open the heavy, panelled door, and went back to the job she had begun with her questioning of careworker Debbie.

There was no one in the corridor, and no one on the magnificent turning staircase that led down to a hall so generous in scale it took a moment to be aware of the reception desk set across part of one side of it. The woman behind it started smiling as Phyllida came into view on the lowest curve, and as Phyllida set foot on the flat she leaned forward with a welcoming gesture. She had been the first member of the Manor staff Phyllida had encountered on her arrival: a rosy-cheeked woman in her forties or fifties with a smile that looked more genuine than her raven-black hair.

"Ah, Mrs Moon!" The voice was refined London. "Coming down for lunch? You can have it upstairs if you prefer, you know."

"I know, but I'd rather come down. I like meeting new people." Which was Phyllida's first lie, telling her it would be accurate, as well as helpful for concentration, to think of herself as once again in character.

"Lovely! I'm Josie Durant, by the way. I'm here on reception during the daytime on weekdays, so if there's anything you want to know, just come and ask me."

She'd said it often before, of course, but Josie Durant still contrived to make it sound personally crafted for Phyllida. Quite an accomplishment. It looked as though the management's recruiting skills were as impressive as the art that had gone into the fitting out of Stansfield Manor: anyone who was subverting the triumphant course of this five-star establishment had to have a great deal of nerve.

"Thank you, you're very kind."

"To the right, just short of the staircase." Josie consulted her watch. "You're a little early, so go past the dining room to the lounge. The double doors at the end."

Phyllida nodded with a smile and set off, aware as she walked of the mingled scent of flowers – there was a small vase of full-blown garden roses on the reception desk and a tall urn with mixed blooms on a turn of the stairs – and expensive soft furnishings. No hint of the smell which had made her fight against retching when she had once visited her father as a temporary resident in a more traditional style of nursing home.

As she passed the open dining-room door

Phyllida glimpsed small tables set with bright glass and cutlery, and then she was moving between the wide double doors of the lounge.

This was the grandest room she had so far entered, but the first to provide visual evidence that Stansfield Manor was neither hotel nor private house. The usual large nursing home circle of armchairs had been broken up into groups of three and four, hotel style, but in front of several of them were individual tables on tubular supports. It was immediately clear to Phyllida, either from the way their owners were sitting or the blankness of their faces, that some of them would be unable to get to the dining room unassisted.

One couple, however, who could have been models for the desirable face of late middle age, were standing in front of the classical chimney piece – the fireplace had been hidden for summer behind an artistic arrangement of dried leaves and flowers in another tall urn. Each of them had a glass of sherry in hand, restoring for an unnerving moment Phyllida's sense of having managed after all to get away on holiday as she had intended...

"Ah! Our newest lady has decided to lunch with us!" She had been unaware of the nurse, now stepping towards her with a professional smile from a corner of the room where an old man sat drowsing. "We're glad to see you, Mrs Moon."

"Thank you." A little frightening, the efficiency at Stansfield Manor, Phyllida found herself thinking, as she put her hand into the one outstretched to her. Everything noted and remembered. How could anyone get away with a misdemeanour as outrageous as murder? Detective Chief Superintendent Kendrick must for once have been misled by the over-reaction of a woman recovering from illness. She should have asked him what had been the matter with his wife's cousin...

"What a lovely room!"

"It is, isn't it?" The nurse gave a satisfied smile as her large pale eyes followed Phyllida's round the lounge. She was wearing the same style of royal blue nursing dress as Sister Caroline, but the contrast between them was far more than physical. In place of her superior's confident gravitas, this shorter, plumper woman struck Phyllida as tense and on edge despite the determined cheeriness of her voice, and there was a perpetual slight frown on her high white brow. "You have a similar view of the garden, Mrs Moon; your room is over part of the drawing room. You can walk in the garden any time you want, you know. Not through the French window, I'm afraid, we keep that locked in case anyone unsteady on their feet should be tempted to go it alone." Perhaps it was that the voice was a little too youthful for someone who had to be in her fifties, and as Sister Anne gave a tinkling little laugh Phyllida was reminded of the voices of actresses in the old black-and-white films she sometimes watched at night. "Now, I'm Anne. I work with – under" – Phyllida was aware of the quick correction – "Sister Caroline; we're both SRNs. So if you have any medical problems please let one of us know. And there is one thing..."

Sister Anne was pale, but her round face flushed a brief pink as she paused and ran her fingers through short dark hair dull from over-perming.

"What can it be?" Phyllida off duty would never have asked so facetious a question, or accompanied it with what she saw in the gilded mirror over the fireplace was a mischievous smile. Yes, she now knew that, as always, she was working in character.

"It's just that we have a rule ... Residents are asked to hand their medication over to Sister Caroline or to me. Totally unnecessary in a case like yours, of course, but we

51

can hardly insist on it for some and not for others. For the less – well – we ask for it on arrival. There was no need for that with you, Mrs Moon, but if you wouldn't mind sometime before this evening, so that when I do the second round of the day I can dispense yours along with the rest."

"Of course. I just have an antibiotic, and some painkillers I don't need regularly any more."

"Fine!" The nurse had visibly relaxed, and Phyllida decided she had been braced for the regular risk of causing offence to those newcomers who expected the hotel ambience to be total. "If you'd like a sherry, by the way ... In the corner cupboard. There's a book to sign on the table underneath. You'll find medium and dry."

"Thank you. I'll enjoy that."

As Phyllida finished speaking, a woman sitting behind a table called out in a fretful voice, "Nurse! When are we going to have something to eat, for God's sake?"

"Any minute now, Mrs Thornton." With an apologetic smile Sister Anne turned away and bent coaxingly over the woman who had questioned her. "Just you hang on."

"It'd be all right if I'd had breakfast!"

"You did have breakfast, Mrs Thornton. Upstairs in your bedroom."

"You're a liar!"

The accusation rang through the calm of the orderly room, disrupting it in one searing instant. Phyllida saw the two people by the fireplace raise eyebrows at one another before both taking a gulp of sherry, and she was aware of one or two of the seated residents shifting in their chairs.

"All right, Mrs Thornton. You'll feel better later."

"I won't!"

This time the nurse turned away without response, and so failed to witness the transformation in the woman's face that was as dramatic in its effect as her shouted complaints. As Phyllida watched her she saw the angry eyes soften, the mouth relax and the furious red recede, and was able to register a rather pretty woman with a polite, puzzled look in eyes she now saw were large and brown. On her mouth was an uncertain smile, and she put out an imploring hand as she spoke again.

"Nurse..."

This time the voice was soft and polite, gently questioning. It made the nurse turn round, but not before Phyllida, on a reflex that for a few seconds overrode her role, had taken a reassuring hold of the hand and received a slight squeeze in return.

"Mrs Thornton..." Gently the nurse took the hand from Phyllida and squatted down beside the woman's chair. "It's all right, you see, it's absolutely all right."

"Yes ... But I'm not sure ... Will Emma be coming this afternoon?"

"I expect so. But you've your lunch to enjoy first. And then a bit of a nap." Sister Anne briefly pressed the hand between both of hers before putting it back in its owner's lap and getting to her feet.

"Yes. Thank you." Mrs Thornton smiled up at her – a lovely smile, Phyllida thought – but as the sister moved on to another occupied chair it disappeared into a brief look of panic before a slight bewilderment set in, which disappeared only as Mrs Thornton closed her eyes with a sigh.

When Phyllida turned to face the room with a glass of dry sherry in her hand Sister Anne was again beside her. "It's very sad," the sister said softly. "In between whiles – for most of the time, so far – Mrs Thornton's fine, she's herself. But then – this comes on."

"Is there something that triggers it?"

"Not that we can find. She's on medication, but very mild because we don't want to affect her normal self adversely."

"I suppose not." A laudable reaction to a

difficult situation. "Does Mrs Thornton live her permanently?"

"Oh, no. It's just while her family's away visiting relatives in Canada. Only for a couple of weeks."

So if someone was wanting to do something, they would have to get on with it. If, of course, Mrs Thornton was eligible for the treatment the Chief Superintendent was afraid might already have been applied twice.

"What is her trouble?" Phyllida asked casually, sipping sherry as she awaited Sister Anne's reply.

"It's unusual for it to come and go like it does with Mrs Thornton, but I'm afraid it's a form of Alzheimer's so it can only get worse. The poor lady also has heart trouble, so we have to hope that will save her from a miserable old age."

A low booming sound from beyond the door greeted Sister Anne's words, an uncanny echo of Phyllida's own reaction to them that made her jerk with the dual shock. "There goes the gong!" the sister announced bracingly to the room. "And here comes Debbie to help us all to get to our lunch!"

Five

I was never again at ease with her – with myself, with anyone – after that terrible moment at the sitting-room window. Although her eyes came back to themselves and were able to communicate with mine in our old unspeaking way, I was forever waiting for my second loss and every precious look we exchanged was tinged with a sort of valedictory sorrow because I knew it might be the last.

It was, in the event, quite some time – weeks if not months – before she disappeared again, but my terror didn't ebb because I knew what I'd seen, and what it had to mean. So now, and always, I regret that I had so little joy in our last true contact...

It was in the night next time. I was deeply asleep, and I think she cried out twice before I was awake and listening, not just hearing a voice which at first had been part of my dream. A bad dream, I remember, almost a nightmare, which was what I awoke to.

"No, no, no, no, no!" I don't know how often she shouted the word. I thought – hoped – at first that she was asleep and it was part of her dream, but when I switched on the bedside lamp I saw that her eyes were wide and staring. I remember I didn't want to speak to her, didn't want her to turn to me, look at me and not see me, which I knew she would do. But I had to comfort her, and I took her in my arms so that her head was on my shoulder and I could postpone for a little while looking into her face.

She didn't struggle against me; she made a sort of nestling movement and I thought she might be coming back to herself. But then she sprang away, stared through me with wild, unseeing eyes, and asked a question in a calm, deep voice.

"Where's Susie?"

It was the worst question she could have asked, a question way beyond my fears at that point of what might be to come, because our daughter Susie died in a road accident when she was fourteen.

"Peggy ... Darling ... Susie isn't with us any more. She left us when she was hit by that car..." To go somewhere else? I have never been able to make up my mind. Peggy, though, had always had faith that her daughter hadn't ceased to exist. But now she had forgotten Susie was dead.

"Susie! I want Susie! Where is she?"

She was frantic, and when she got to the point of struggling so hard that I would have hurt her by restraining her I let go, and she flung out of bed – only to stagger round to my side, flop down against me, and lift the receiver from the telephone on my bedside table.

I suppose I could have wrestled it from her, but I'd had enough of fighting her, and anyway there was a part of me that wanted to know the worst, wanted to know the range and extent of her madness. There was something else, too: I thought she would be ringing a member of her family, who were her best friends as well as her kin, and the last few moments had brought me to the knowledge that the time had come for me to share with them what was befalling her. So far I had said nothing, they had said nothing, and I assumed she had shown no symptoms in company other than mine. It would be a cruel way, I knew, for one of them to learn the direction in which she was going. Far kinder to have a warning word from me – but at least whoever was to receive her call would have no difficulty believing what I would tell them.

If, that is, she was able to punch out a number correctly. I knew that it was a possibility: I knew the case of a woman who had been assigned to an EMI home by unanimous decision of senior psychiatrists, doctors and nurses, and who for several months after her committal continued to play a fair game of bridge...

I watched Peggy's hands – unerring, and giving me a searing pang in my chest when I contrasted their efficiency with the state of the rest of her – and saw that she was ringing her brother Robert, which would have been my guess. She and Robert – the Golden Pair, cherished but unenvied, I had always suspected, by their less physically attractive siblings – were nearest in age and had from childhood, I had been regularly informed, had a particular bond. Sometimes I vaguely wonder if that was why he has never married, but I have no reason for speculating about this. And Robert seems fond enough of women; it's only that he has never settled for just one.

It was a quarter past four in the morning, and it took some time for the ringing tone to cut out. I heard the cross voice at the other end start a sleepy question and then Peggy broke into it with a fierce question of her own.

"Where's Susie? Robert, you've got to tell me! Eric won't say, I think he's keeping us apart, I think he doesn't want her to see me. Her own mother! Robert, you've got to help me! D'you know where she is?"

There was no immediate answer, which didn't surprise me. I was feeling more and more sorry for Robert, and I put out a reflex hand to the telephone receiver. To my surprise Peggy let me take it from her, and curled up with a sob in the small space on the side of the bed. I knew, somehow, that whatever I said to Robert, she wouldn't hear it.

"Robert? It's Eric. I'm so very sorry. There's started to be – some signs ... But nothing like this, tonight. I tried to stop her but she was very strong..."

"And now?" There was scarcely a wobble in Robert's voice. But they're a tough lot, all of them.

"She let me take the phone and she's curled up small beside me. Not asleep, but not aware. She'll probably wake in the morning without remembering any of this, and knowing Susie's dead."

"Why for God's sake haven't you spoken to us?"

"I've told you, there's been nothing, really, to say. If she hadn't rung you now I'd have told you tomorrow – all of you – that she was asking for Susie. It's ... It's getting worse."

"Good God, man." There had been other times when I'd sensed I was exasperating Robert, but he'd never shown it openly, like this. "Getting worse? It has to be as bad as it could be!"

"Not till now." For once I didn't feel I had to handle one of them with care; now Peggy was the only thing that was important. "Come round in the morning if you want to. With any of the others. Will you tell them?"

"I'll tell them. And *I'll* come round now!"

"*No!*" I had never so openly opposed him. Opposed any of them. "Leave it till the morning. She's gone to sleep."

She had. When Robert had reluctantly agreed to wait until a civilised time and I had rung off, I put the bedclothes round her and then rolled as gently as I could over to her side, where I lay facing her until I heard the papers arrive, my hand on her waist. Then I got out of bed, went round to my side, and very gently eased her across to her own place. She didn't stir, but when the postman wrestled a large package through the slot and it fell with a thud on to the vestibule tiles she yawned and stretched, opened her eyes and smiled at me.

61

"Good morning, my darling," she said, holding out her arms. "Let's not get up just yet, shall we?"

I remember feeling sick with regret that the family was on its way.

Six

Following Sister Anne's announcement of lunch, Debbie and the younger girl at her heels made a beeline for the old man by the window. As they hauled him slowly to his feet, one on each side of him, Sister Anne bent over a woman who needed only one strong arm to hoist her up. These were the first stages of a gentle but strict routine that would get all the downstairs lunchers into the dining room as speedily and efficiently as possible. In less than ten minutes everyone was seated next door and awaiting the first of what the cutlery told Phyllida were three courses, the most frail grouped together at the two tables nearest to the door.

Phyllida was invited to a table in one of the two window corners, and was reminded of the system on the large liner where early in their marriage she and Gerald had taken an unrepeatably stressful job as entertainers. There had been no classes, but the people in the superior cabins had taken their meals in the superior of the two restaurants...

It was a table for four, and the couple who had been drinking sherry by the fireplace were already seated on the chairs that faced the garden. Phyllida waited while a white-haired woman with an apologetic smile performed the wriggle necessary to get herself into one of the inner seats, then followed suit into the other, rejoicing that the couple's enjoyment of the outdoors had left her able to observe what was going on inside.

"We're George and Greta Howard," the man said in a serious tone, as Phyllida spread a crisp white napkin over her knees.

"I'm Phyllida Moon." How extraordinary to be at work for Peter, and saying those three revealing words! For a moment it made her feel cold, and a goose walked over her grave.

"Are you all right, Mrs Moon?" The white-haired lady had noted the shudder, and was surveying her with concern.

Phyllida managed a laugh. "I'm fine, thanks. It's only about ten days since I lost my gall bladder, and I seem to be a bit fragile still."

"Of course you do! Lost mine ten years or so ago, and I felt very fragile indeed!" Greta Howard, who looked the archetypal healthy

Chair of some green-wellie committee, nodded understandingly. "But you'll be right as rain in no time, you'll see."

"Thanks; I hope so. In the meantime, this seems like a very good place to recover in." She was continuing, Phyllida discovered to her wary surprise, to react like someone other than herself, which must mean that her characters were only partly dependent on their physical trappings. It was an interesting discovery, and one which gave her a brief flash of satisfaction that she was still capable of extending her thespian skills – the only part of herself for which she was ever able to entertain approval.

"It certainly is. Best hotel anywhere around." George Howard announced his opinion with the same earnest solemnity with which he had endowed his announcement of his and his wife's names. "Glad of an excuse to come here."

"You shouldn't say that, dear. Health is all." Greta Howard's rebuke was kindly. "He's had a little hernia op," she told Phyllida. "So why should I stay at home alone?"

"Why indeed," responded Phyllida Mark Two, "when you too can enjoy the first-class hotel?"

"How right you are! And George is fine; he only needs a bit of a rest."

"That's good." Phyllida spoke automatically as she turned to face the other woman at the table. The Howards hadn't even glanced at her, directing all their remarks exclusively to Phyllida, whose modesty was happy to be able to put this down to her status of newcomer, coupled perhaps with the comparatively extrovert nature of the *alter ego* which had brought itself into being that day. "I hope that's all you need, too, Mrs ... ?"

"Anderson. Doris Anderson." The woman offered Phyllida a brief grateful smile. She was small and round with a pretty pink and white face, and looked to be in her early eighties. Phyllida had taken to her on sight. "Yes, really, thank you. My daughter ... I haven't been too well lately, and now I'm enjoying a rest at this lovely place. Ah, vegetable soup! I think it's my favourite here."

The soup, Phyllida agreed after one mouthful, was very good: packed with its title ingredient and lacking the floury content which too often dominates restaurant soups announced as "cream of". She was surprised to find herself hungry for the first time in six queasy weeks, and able to proceed to the ensuing chicken casserole with scarcely diminished appetite. Pudding, though, was something she had long grown unaccustomed to, and in company with the other two women she settled for fruit from the bowl set down in the centre of the table when George Howard was served his rhubarb crumble.

"Is the evening meal as substantial?" Phyllida inquired, as she decided to wipe the juice off her fingers with a tissue from her bag rather than the still pristine napkin.

"I don't think it's quite——"

"No." Mrs Howard's robust tones cut out Mrs Anderson's gentle voice with such total effect that Mrs Anderson stopped speaking and looked down at her plate. She managed a glance at Phyllida, however, which Phyllida acknowledged with an infinitesimal shrug of the shoulders that, she rightly gauged, would escape the Howards' unsubtle beams. "It's another excellent meal," Mrs Howard went on, "but it's supper, so it's a bit lighter. Served far too early, of course, but at least at the Manor they don't call it tea." Greta Howard's glance as she shuddered lit for the first time, briefly, on Doris Anderson, and Phyllida decided it must be the trace of a Northern intonation in Mrs Anderson's voice that had made her *persona non grata* with the Howards.

"I see," she murmured, starting to wonder what she would do with her first afternoon.

The sherry and the size of the meal were already telling her that a nap would be her personal option, and she tried to reprove her sense of satisfaction that her surgeon had made her promise to lie on her bed after lunch for at least an hour. Beyond that hour, though, there stretched a long unstructured time. If she had been in the character of a woman with mental illness, Phyllida reflected, she could have wandered into all sorts of places without arousing suspicion. But if Mr Kendrick's friend was right about what had been happening at the Manor, that could have been the last thing she did...

Peter was off on an investigation that would take the whole day, so it was unlikely there would be a telephone call and even if he had been around he couldn't have risked a visit. What Debbie had told her could be significant and she was anxious to pass it on to him, but they would both want to discuss it and his mobile, perhaps answered in the company of others, was not the best medium. So she must hold it until the night, and when she had had her rest she must go down into the lounge and get into conversation. She was already confident that Mrs Moon would be able to do what was not in her own nature: chat people up.

"What do you tend to do in the afternoons?" she asked Mrs Anderson. She wanted to break through what had clearly before her arrival been the little lady's isolation without offending the Howards – since starting to work for Peter, Phyllida had learned that detectives need all the inadvertent allies they can get – and they had begun to talk in low tones exclusively to one another.

"Me?" After an initial slight surprise, Doris Anderson smiled. "I'm afraid I go to bed. Well, not entirely. I mean, I take my shoes off and lie under the bedspread. Just for an hour or so. Then ... Well, on a day like today I walk in the garden. It's beautiful, you know. If you're at all interested, there are all sorts of lovely things you can't see from the windows. And there are seats here and there, so that you can tuck yourself into a sheltered corner and find yourself going to sleep again! I'm afraid—"

"An excellent planting policy!" Greta Howard cut in, speaking to Phyllida. "But that's to be expected, seeing that when the Manor opened as a nursing home the owners had the garden redesigned by staff from our local Botanic Gardens."

"Ah ... Didn't I hear the Director had been promoted to Edinburgh?" She couldn't help it. And in her own persona it was all right;

the staff of the Manor knew Phyllida Moon lived locally, her home address was in the register of temporary residents.

The thought of it there brought the goose waddling back, and a second concerned look from Doris Anderson.

"That's right," George Howard contributed, unnoticing. "New chap's very young, but my wife says he'll do. She's the expert in the garden department." He might be top drawer socially, but Phyllida would have liked to see his hand disguise a yawn so wide it would have given her a good view of his rear dental work if she hadn't looked away. "Well, I'm for the afternoon siesta!"

"And I'm for a good long walk!" Greta Howard's eye fell speculatively on Phyllida, who for the first time was grateful to the uncultivated fragility which made even so unsubtle an observer as Mrs Howard turn her gaze away with a little frown of frustration. It would have been amusing to see her reaction if Mrs Anderson had volunteered herself as a walking companion, but she could only have made the suggestion as a masochist or a joker, and although Phyllida thought there was evidence of a sense of humour at the corners of her mouth and in her blue eyes, it would hardly take her so far.

"See you this evening, then, if not before!" Greta Howard said to Phyllida as she and her husband rose from the table. Several of the able-bodied had already left, Phyllida noted as the Howards crossed the room. She had also noted, with approval, that either Debbie or the other young girl had remained in constant attendance during the meal on the two tables where the incapacitated residents had been seated.

"They're awfully good here, you know." It was as if Doris Anderson had read her thoughts. Phyllida gave another small start, then hoped Mrs Anderson wouldn't think she had a tic. Without the protective shell of a physical disguise she should be taking even more care than usual to contain her reactions. She was at work, and she must pull herself together.

"I'm off to bed for an hour. Doctor's orders." Phyllida sprang to her feet in her usual way, then had to steady herself against the table until the dizziness had passed.

At work? Smiling reassuringly into Doris Anderson's concerned face, Phyllida bowed to the reminder that she really was a patient in a nursing home recovering from surgery, and that this might explain her self-discipline lagging behind her reactions, as well as her physical weakness. Work, currently, was

71

a secondary occupation; her first was to get well. Even the Chief Superintendent would have to list the priorities of her stay at the Manor in that order.

"You better go and lie down!" Debbie told her sternly as Phyllida tottered past her.

"I'm on my way."

Determining to be sensible, she reluctantly summoned the gilded, lattice-gated lift which had to be contemporary with the elegant appliance in the Agency building, and was swayed slowly to the first floor. Having on this mission no physical secrets, she stayed the usual reflex of her hand to lock her door and stood for a moment with her back against it, enjoying the sense of elegant calm the room conveyed before kicking off her shoes and crossing the yellow shafts of sunshine to the window to tinker with the curtains until the bed was in shade. Then she slid under the coverlet, and was instantly asleep.

Back at the lunch table, she was smiling at Mrs Anderson, who was smiling too until her face distorted with hideous slowness into terror and distress and a great wail of anguish came from her open mouth. Phyllida turned in horror to the Howards, and they were nodding "I told you so", looking smugly at her, and then at each other. Behind Mrs Anderson the garden was the featureless blue-black of night, and a group of people in white coats, headed by the Senior Sister, was crossing the room towards the table, grim determination in every face. Phyllida saw all the Manor staff she had so far encountered before forcing herself against an invisible barrier to lean across the table and lay a finger on Mrs Anderson's howling mouth. She felt the sting of spittle as she begged her to be quiet. "For your own salvation!" The words came out at the top of her voice, and the advancing phalanx faltered. But Mrs Anderson went on screaming, and the grim approach was resumed.

Phyllida tried to shout again but no more words would come, and anyway she had to bring her arm away because of the dreadful pain in it. As she fell back in her chair the Senior Sister reached the table and seized the arm in an agonising grip, her face like thunder. Phyllida made one huge painful effort, and heard the vast "No!" emerging like a gale-force wind that swept everyone and everything out into the darkness. Her last sight was of the Senior Sister's white apron crackling upwards, and then she was lying on her back in bed, the vibrations of her shout still ringing in her ears, feeling for the arm she had been lying on – the source of her dream pain as pins and needles had begun to invade the numbness. Following her operation she had been ordered to sleep on her back, and this was the first time she had reverted to her side – without, it appeared, getting it quite right.

Her hand was still so dead Phyllida hung it over the edge of the bed to encourage the blood flow while the nightmare slowly receded. She felt shaken by it, but managed eventually to be amused by its melodrama and to tell herself that to let its atmosphere persist would be as silly as feeling there was danger in your own life because you'd been watching something spooky on television. There had been times, though, she recalled reluctantly, when a dream she had had during an investigation had turned out to be a reflection of something absorbed by her subconscious...

Far too early for that to be the case now! And too absurd, at any time, to imagine that all the people serving the Manor, from the Director to the most junior careworker, were part of a conspiracy to destroy the aged and infirm.

In any case, Doris Anderson was neither. By the time she was free of the dream's influence, Phyllida had decided it had been generated by no more than the sense she had received at the lunch table of Mrs Anderson being a victim of social exclusion.

Distrusting sleep for that afternoon at least, she was sorry as well as surprised to see that less than half an hour had gone by since she had come up to her room, and as she obediently closed her eyes again she felt wary. But when the telephone rang by her bed she saw from the clock beside it that this time she had been dreamlessly asleep for more than her statutory time.

Anxiety flooded back as she seized the receiver.

"Yes?"

"Mrs Moon? You have a visitor."

Phyllida's life in Seaminster, in either of its manifestations, had not encouraged the making of local friends. As a member of the theatre company with which she had first arrived, her friends (and her enemies) had all been inside the company. Her husband and one or two others, who went more regularly than she did to the favoured bar which Gerald and his crony the producer had sussed out early on in their stay, had made some outside acquaintances, but Phyllida had tended to spend her free time with one or two women friends within the company, or in the long solitary walks during which she had come to terms with the fact that her marriage was over. She had started to work for the Peter Piper Agency soon after she had waved Gerald and the rest of the theatre company goodbye – merely, at first, to get hands-on experience for her role as a PI in the TV series – and her growing involvement there had been even less conducive to getting to know local people in her own persona. The characters she assumed on duty had gained her a wide circle of acquaintance professionally, all of which she had lost the moment the characters ceased to exist. This was the down side of the job she loved: several times it had caused her more than social regret and, of course, it was the reason she had booked her visit to Edinburgh. Outside work she had been so protective of her own persona – her ultimate disguise – that the only people she had got to know had been some members of the staff of the public library (where she worked, when she found time, on her long-ongoing history of women and the stage) and her colleagues at the Agency.

"Who is it?" It was absurd, but the receiver was trembling in her hand.

"It's a Miss Sally Hargreaves."

"Ah! Will you ask her to come up?"

No, of course, she hadn't lost all the

acquaintances she had made in character. Pleasure and relief flooding through her, Phyllida tumbled off the bed and into the bathroom, where she splashed cool water on to her face and shook out her hair. She had been forced to reveal herself to Sally to save the girl's life and there was, of course, no going back. Not that she had wanted to; when she had stopped feeling paranoid and accepted that Sally and her family would keep her secret she had been glad of this bright new friend.

Whom she ought to have told she was going into hospital, Phyllida realised ruefully as she brushed her teeth. She was so unused to friendships outside work she wasn't doing all she should to maintain this one, and she was lucky that Sally was friend enough to make the effort for both of them. She'd do better in the future, Phyllida vowed as she heard the tap on her door: she didn't want to lose Sally.

She started to run across the room, but a fresh wave of dizziness forced her to stop and lean against a chair. As the tap came again she shouted to Sally to come in, and was able to meet her in the doorway.

"Sally! Oh, you're more than I deserve!"

Their arms went out at the same moment and they hugged one another.

"You should have told me!" Sally's reproach was gentle. "I rang you at home a couple of times, then the Agency. Jenny told me where you were."

"I know I should. It's just that I lead such an odd life I don't always do things the way I'd like to if I was ... well, just me."

"But you really are just you now, aren't you?"

"Of course." Phyllida was so schooled in deception she was able to meet Sally's eyes with conviction in her own.

"And of course I believe you. But having said that ... I still can't help wondering if you're working as well as convalescing." Sally laughed at her own absurdity as she looked round the room. "This is something, Phyllida!"

"I know. I was a bit uncomfortable at first, but Peter insisted I had the works, and gave me a bonus so that I could afford it. And as for working, you can check with the hospital that I left my gall bladder there."

"I'll take your word for it. Oh, but it's good to see you!" But Sally's cheerful gaze darkened as her eyes stayed on Phyllida's face. "Though I'd rather see you looking better. The Manor doesn't seem to have done much for you so far."

"I've only just arrived. So I haven't walked

yet in that gorgeous garden." Sally had skipped over to the window and was looking out. "Shall we go and explore?"

"Yes!" Sally clapped her hands as she turned to face Phyllida. "You won't need a jacket, it's so warm. But before we go, you'd better tell me what you do for a living, so that I don't put my foot in it. Have you let on about *A Policeman's Lot*?"

"Heavens, no. I'm a resting actress who's writing a book about women and the stage. All true, at this precise moment. Jenny'll have told you I'm Mrs Moon, I hope. Even in these enlightened days that tends to be a hedge against questions."

"She told me, and that's who I asked for. Now I want to ask you all about your time in London. So let's go!"

Sally offered her arm and Phyllida took it without comment. That was how they slowly descended the stairs, exchanged smiles with Josie Durant, and walked through a door at the back of the hall, which brought them out in the centre of a stone terrace. A few shallow steps led down on to the south-sloping lawn, which was edged immediately below the terrace with a curving stone path that continued down the garden to either side, marching with the borders.

The Director and the doctor had walked

on the grass but Phyllida and Sally took the path to the right, and when they came to the first enclave, with pauses to exclaim at the magnificence of the wide herbaceous border, Sally led the way into it and drew Phyllida down beside her on a wooden seat which was as elegantly made and maintained as any of the Manor's indoor furniture.

"Thanks, Sally. Look, I'm not pretending I'm absolutely recovered. But I haven't had any more pain or sickness, and I ate an enormous lunch."

"I'm glad to hear it. Now, I want a chronological account of the filming. Did you meet anyone special?"

"Not in the sense I think you mean." Phyllida smiled into the searching eyes.

"Don't tell me there wasn't someone who wanted to be."

"That doesn't count. Sorry, Sally." No one would be told about her forays into the Botanic Gardens, or the reason for the visit to Edinburgh – still hanging in the balance – unless they bore fruit. "What about you and Jeremy? All well?"

"Of course. I haven't seen you in the library since you got back from London." Sally was in charge of the lending section, and Phyllida always put her head in before climbing the second flight of stairs to the reference library.

"Because I haven't managed to get there. I'm afraid the book's hanging fire just now, but at least it's useful if people insist on asking me what I do for a living."

"Which you're not doing at the moment."

"I've told you." But voices could be heard approaching, and Sally had to have been aware of the reflex switch to professionalism which Phyllida knew had been visible in the tensing of her body and her suddenly listening stance. "A good habit that's hard to kick," she said softly, in answer to the scepticism of Sally's look. "You can hardly expect me to suddenly—"

She broke off as two shadows appeared along the grass at the entrance to the enclave. Two people walking back up the garden, the sun in the southern sky behind them.

"... knows what he's doing. It worries me."

"You worry too much. About the wrong things, perhaps. *Who* did you say you hope knows what he's doing?"

"All right, Sister. I hope Douglas knows what he's doing."

Phyllida recognised the light, anxious male voice before the Director came into view, alongside the Senior Sister.

"Of course he does. That's one thing—" The contrasting contralto ceased abruptly as the walkers turned into the enclave and saw the silent women on the seat.

"Ah," the Director resumed, less fretfully. "Mrs ... Moon! And a young friend!"

"Yes. What a lovely garden!" Phyllida fancied it was Sister Caroline who looked the more gratified, but her serious, impassive countenance was difficult to read. "But I found this was as far down as I could get without a stop."

"You mustn't be discouraged; it's early days." The Director was looking through her as he spoke and Phyllida thought the words came off the top of his head, a useful comforter that would fit an unscheduled encounter with the majority of the patients at the Manor and require no interruption to whatever was preoccupying him.

There was another seat further into the enclave, and with a smile Phyllida gestured towards it.

"Thank you, but we must get back to our duties. Enjoy the sunshine!"

"Thank you. We will. I enjoyed my lunch too, Sister."

"Good." Both gave a slight bow of acknowledgement before turning away, and as she put her finger to her lips and listened to the silence, Phyllida thanked fate that she was with the one person outside her work in front of whom she could make the gesture and be afraid of no more than a teasing, "I knew I was right!"

Seven

I made sure I first saw the members of the family without Peggy being present. This entailed getting swiftly to the front door four times, as they of course didn't arrive together (although I had had an absurd mental picture of the lot of them bunched up on the front step).

George arrived first, and I was relieved to see that he was without the complication of his wife (Mona by name, and by nature, too): the family is formidable enough without its contingent of husbands, wives and offspring. Robert came alone, of course, a few minutes after George, as did Pamela. Freda and Freddie, the last arrivals, appeared to have met at the gate.

So there we were. Peggy's eldest brother George, a blackly hairy patriarchal figure, head and eldest member of the family and never for a moment forgetting it; Golden Boy Robert trying to maintain his usual lazy stance but giving away his anxiety – to me, at least – via the tic under an eye and restless movements about the room. Freda and Freddie looking at Peggy in poorly disguised dismay – the only thing, I thought as I regarded them, that they had in common apart from their slender height: Freda is so calm and elegant, and Freddie so gauche and awkward with his unruly hair and great lump of Adam's apple forever jerking about his long throat as he bumps into furniture and knocks crockery off tables. He knocked his cup over that morning, fortunately after he had emptied it. And Pamela, the most humourless of a clan not noted for its humour, and superficially at least the strongest and coolest, although as an ageing spinster she could, for all I know, be a smouldering cauldron ... well, Pamela, of course, despite my suggestion of soft-pedalling, had gone striding over to Peggy, sat down beside her and taken possession of her hand.

I remember I had never been so aware of what a strange pair of twins Freda and Freddie are: the youngest members of the family, so that Peggy, who comes between George and Robert, had been able to tell me that Freda's dominance had begun in early childhood, when she had always been that bit quicker than Freddie and he had been content to accept it, sit back, and let her do things for both of them. They went their own ways when they grew up, but Freddie didn't marry and Freda chose a compliant husband. Not, I feel compelled in fairness to add here, that Freda is a dominant personality in general – no, we leave that to Pamela – only so far as Freddie is concerned. In fact Freda, of them all, is the nearest to being detached, and chose a complaisant husband because, I believe, of being at heart a free spirit rather than because of wanting to be in control.

I remember how my own heart ached as I watched Peggy, looking from one to the other of us in affectionate bemusement. Her recovery had continued through our love-making (although my fear that it might not had made the proceedings less than successful, a failure my darling Peggy had teased away with loving hands), our dressing, our breakfast in the sunny kitchen window, and our turning to face the day. I had known this was possible, I knew the recovery might continue for days or even weeks, and I had hoped it would be Robert alone who came to call at my stipulated hour of ten and no earlier. But the moment I saw George's dark, wavy-edged silhouette through the figured glass of the vestibule door I realised how naïve that hope had been. Anything approaching a family crisis – and what could be more critical than this? – demands them all.

I had told each of them in the hall that all was temporarily well, and begged them in a whisper not to show their anxiety. Before anyone arrived I had suggested to Peggy that she might like to work on her embroidery frame, the light was so good, in the hope that when the front door bell first sounded she would decide there was no point in trying to extricate herself from behind it when I was already on my feet. Thus I would have the chance to tell whoever turned up that she was "herself", and to be "themselves" likewise. I was afraid Robert might use the key he had never given back, but he had the grace, that morning, to ring the bell with the rest of them.

"What's all this for?" Peggy asked reasonably. "Have I forgotten someone's anniversary?" I remember she turned to me and looked into my eyes with total normality. "I know it isn't ours, darling."

George terrified me by clearing his throat, his usual procedure before embarking on some gnomic utterance, and I lurched into what I had decided I would tell her in explanation if she was still seeing the world straight. "It's just a little surprise, darling.

We haven't met together, all of us, for such a long time, and when Robert pointed that out to me yesterday" – I was grateful for the fact that he and I sometimes come across one another at work – "I suggested they pop in this morning for coffee." I was grateful, too, that it was a Sunday, and I remember thinking that even in so dreadful a situation the fates seemed to be with us, Peggy and me. "The logical next step was to get in touch with Freda and Freddie and George, and ... here they are!"

"I hope their respective spouses won't be sulking, darling."

The old Peggy! My adored, sweet-natured, witty wife!

"They were invited as well, my darling. But I suppose with Sunday morning being so vital for getting home things done..."

"Mona was coming," George announced. "But then she realised how much baking she has to do for her WI coffee morning tomorrow and asked to be excused. You know how conscientious she is." And something of a reformed rake, Peggy had told me once, with a wicked grin; Mona was said to have rattled around a bit before she met the upright George, and her righteousness according to my wife was the righteousness of the converted sinner.

With most people I know, I would have taken George's little tale as a piece of tact, but I was aware that with George and Mona it was likely to be the truth. (I learned later that it was.) Freda then offered a vague excuse for her other half, and Peggy appeared to accept them both. But of course she turned to me and reproved me mildly for not having given her the chance of ensuring there was plenty of fresh coffee, and biscuits in the barrel.

"But maybe I'm underestimating you, Eric. Maybe you looked after these things yourself?"

I hadn't looked after them, of course; the family hadn't given me time. But I had looked into the coffee jar and the biscuit barrel after breakfast when she had left the kitchen, and seen they were sufficiently well stocked for there to be no need of an SOS to one or more of her siblings to bring something I could smuggle into the kitchen.

"Yes, darling," I responded smugly. "I did."

"Thank you." She got to her feet. As lithe as always, but then it was only – *only!* – her brain that was suffering.

"I'll come with you," Pamela said of course, rising too.

Fortunately Peggy had already reached

the door, and I was able to take hold of Pamela's arm and whisper in her ear to promise me to act naturally.

With a bad grace she did, but I was still agonisingly uneasy.

George, of course, the moment the sitting-room door swung to behind them, cleared his throat again.

"So, Eric," he demanded. "What is to be done?"

I remember Freda, who had been absorbed in the intricacies of Peggy's stitching, turning towards me and languidly echoing the question. Robert and Freddie were watching me with interest, but, to their credit, they are not so inclined as Pamela and George to tell other people how to conduct themselves.

"Nothing!" I responded sternly, relieved to discover that the new me who had opposed Robert over the telephone had reappeared. I had not been at all certain that he would return, despite my determination not to let Peggy be treated as an invalid before it became absolutely necessary. "We do nothing," I repeated firmly. "Last night was an aberration. All that has happened so far is that now and then – not often – she gets ... well, lost, frightened ... The worst thing then is that she doesn't – see people.

Doesn't see *me*." I managed not to let those last words come out like the wail of an abandoned baby, but it was difficult.

"What do you mean?" asked Freda, with interest rather than pity or sorrow, moving her gaze to the mirror above the embroidery frame and patting her hair. But I have always felt that both the twins lack empathy to an even greater extent than their siblings.

"I mean ... For a moment she can only see inward visions, terrifying ones, and people – outside – aren't individuals, they're just – agents, she hopes, of her salvation. Oh, that sounds nonsense, but it's as near as I can get. And it *is* only moments. I know it will get worse" – I remember how it hurt to put that inevitability into words – "but the time isn't here yet. I'm not sorry she got through to Robert last night, it was time you knew – and I kept hoping you'd see for yourselves – but that doesn't mean I'm suggesting we take any action. Well, the very fact that you haven't seen for yourselves shows how little it's taken hold so far..."

To my surprise and chagrin, at that moment I began to cry. Robert stepped forward, and to my further surprise put his arms around me and gave me a hug. "Bear up!" he whispered in my ear. "She'll be coming in soon, and what can you say to her if you're in tears?"

"Thanks, Robert." He has always been the one I dislike least. "You're right." And with another supreme effort I blew my nose and shook the tears away, so that when Peggy and Pamela came in with the coffee a moment or so later I knew I at least appeared composed.

I could see that everyone was covertly eyeing her performance, watching to see if her hand trembled, or her eyes went wild. It was inevitable, after what I had told them, and it was illogical of me to despise them for it – I was doing it myself, now, all the time – but I couldn't help it, couldn't help thinking of them as our enemies, Peggy's and mine. Yet she was one of them, and needed them as they needed her.

When Peggy had poured second cups of coffee all round, Freddie started to hum. Tunelessly. A thing he does when he's worried or upset. So of course Peggy asked him if there was anything wrong.

"Oh, Pegs! I can't ... No, of course not. Why d'you ask?"

"Because you were singing, chump."

"Was I? I can't think why. Everything's – fine."

"I'm glad to hear it, little brother." Fortunately Peggy looked down at the tray as she spoke, so that she missed the eye-rolling Freddie directed around at the rest of us.

What an impossible fellow!

But one mustn't speak ill of the dead.

Eight

It had been agreed with the Chief Superintendent that Phyllida would maintain contact only via the Agency, and when Sally had gone – unable to tease out of her friend any verbal acknowledgement that she was currently a sleuth as well as a convalescent, but dancing off with a look of sly triumph that Phyllida continued to be confident she had no need to worry about – Phyllida rang the office without much hope, and found that Peter had just got there.

"I was amazingly lucky in one way," she told him, when he had talked out his disappointment that his own operation had been aborted, and she had reported the encounter in the garden. "I missed the first name the Director said by a whisker, but I heard the second one loud and clear. The odds must be in favour of its being the same as the first, but there was just something in the way he offered it that made me wonder if perhaps Sister Caroline had administered a reproof and he was making a correction. But that's total speculation."

"I've learned to listen to your speculations."

"Don't put too much on this one. And if I'm right, what possible significance can it have? Sister Caroline spoke in a relaxed, neutral sort of voice all the time, but the Director sounded – well, bothered. From what I saw of him when I arrived, though, that could just be because he tends by nature to look on life as the enemy."

"Fair enough. Douglas?"

"No member of staff with the name, first or surname, according to the brochure."

"I suppose it could be the first or second name of someone belonging to a resident."

"I suppose it could." Phyllida looked at her watch. "There's an hour to go before the evening meal. I'll go downstairs now and try to talk to the woman who went off her trolley suddenly just before lunch. She seemed to get back on it just as abruptly – nothing untoward in the dining room. And Sister Anne – she's the qualified nurse under the Senior Sister – told me she comes and goes."

"Alzheimer's?"

"Form of. Sister Anne also told me she has heart trouble."

"Did she, now! Preparing the ground?"

"If there really is something sinister going on."

"Anything else?"

"The careworker who first took me to my room – name of Debbie – is a natural chatterbox and seems to have taken to Mrs Moon, which could be useful."

"You make her sound like one of your characters. Mrs Moon, I mean."

"Peter, she is! Not just because she never existed – my married name was Waterhouse, which I've probably never bothered to tell you – and I know it's me who's getting over an operation – but ... this Mrs Moon *isn't* me. For a start, she's more outgoing and doesn't have any difficulty starting conversations and making silly little jokes and generally being – another woman!"

"Interesting. No, really. I wasn't expecting to hear this."

"I wasn't expecting to say it. It *is* interesting. I'm especially intrigued to find I can take on a character without any props."

"I'm not as surprised as you are, because I know you're so clever." There was a fractional pause before Peter continued on a rush. "Oh, God, Phyllida, how are *you*? *Miss Moon*? That's the first question I should've asked."

"I'm all right. Truly. Good food, rest – I'll be lying down every afternoon and having breakfast in bed – gentle walks. One thing: Sally Hargreaves came to see me this afternoon, and was around when I – when I went into work mode as we overheard Sister Caroline and Dr Hartley."

"But you're not worried."

"No. I know Sally. She knows, without my having admitted it, that there's something on, but she'd die rather than tell anyone, even her partner."

"If you're not worried about Sally, I'm not. I'm glad you had her company this afternoon."

"Thanks. Peter, the room is sumptuous. Kendrick has really pushed my boat out."

"He's celebrating having solved the riddle of the Sphinx. I think it got to him."

"It may get to him again next time I put on a new skin. But yes, I think he does believe at the moment that you have only one female operator in the field. Now, I'll go downstairs and try to do some work."

Before leaving her room Phyllida went across to the window and gazed down the garden. The strength was leaving the sun, and the colour scheme below was fading slowly to pastel. Wisps of cirrus stretched across the paling sky, tipped with gold from a sun out of sight towards the west but still sending fingers of light, now almost horizontal, across the lower reaches of the lawn. Two small groups of residents and visitors were walking on the stone paths, one to either side and both pausing to point out and admire particular blooms in the herbaceous borders. Phyllida watched idly, the peace of the scene evoking a mournful sense of the unattained peace she had hoped to find for herself when she visited the Botanic Gardens – and then, after that disappointment, when she went to Edinburgh...

And was still hoping to find, she realised on a stab of anger at her own stupidity. Life was good, now, as it was, and she must stop courting frustration and despair, which was all her absurd quest could lead to. It was a relief to see Debbie emerging from an enclave with a resident on her arm, and to welcome the swift metamorphosis into Mrs Moon, who had no feelings, of sorrow or of joy.

Just before she disappeared from sight under Phyllida's window Debbie glanced up, and her face split into a huge smile as she waved a hand. An ally there, Phyllida thought as she turned away after responding, and one who was unlikely to sense nuances while being asked questions because she would always be too busy getting ready for her own next burst of talk.

Unless *she* was in disguise, as part of a sinister establishment?

Phyllida warned herself against paranoia with a quelling glare into the bathroom mirror as she tidied her hair, then left the room with as near as she could manage to her old swift pace, descended the grand staircase and continued on into the lounge.

Here, for the moment, all appeared quiet and relaxed. The woman who had been so disturbed before lunch was sitting alone, her chair slightly turned towards the main window so that she appeared to be staring down the garden. With a few smiles to right and left Phyllida threaded between the other armchairs and the tables, sat down in the chair nearest to the solitary woman, and edged it forward until she was just within her possible field of vision. There was no reaction as she settled herself, and when she looked into the woman's face the staring eyes remained fixed on the far horizon.

But Phyllida had learned that the farther a fixed gaze appeared to be focused, the more likely it was to be looking inward, into the watcher's own mind.

"Hello," she said softly. "I'm Phyllida

Moon. Isn't it a lovely garden?"

Slowly, very slowly, the gaze shortened, the eyes softened, and when the woman turned her head to meet Phyllida's they offered normal contact. "Yes," she said. "Lovely." For a moment her face was perplexed, but it cleared as Phyllida smiled. "I'm Angela Thornton." She looked tired and washed out, her grey-streaked hair lifeless and her skin strained across the bones of her face, but there was still an impression of underlying strength which made Phyllida decide she could be scarcely into her sixties.

"Well. Hello, Angela!" Miss Moon would never have said *that*, and Phyllida was reassured that she was safely in character. "This is a lovely place altogether, isn't it?"

"Yes. Yes, it is." Again the flash of perplexity.

"Have you been here long?"

"No. And I'm soon going home."

Something in the way she offered the information told Phyllida that Angela Thornton was quoting: the reassuring words of a family who didn't feel able to cope with increasing forays into dementia.

"That's good. So am I. But it's not at all bad being here, is it?"

"No." A mild curiosity had entered the

inexpressive eyes. "Are you ... ? I mean ... Is that why you're here? Have your people gone away too? My daughter'll be gone in a day or two. She and her husband have had an invitation from my brother in Canada."

So that was how her family were doing it, giving themselves time to think things through in a wider context while discovering how their mother, or grandmother, or both, reacted to life in a home.

"I'm not so lucky, Mrs Thornton." Despite the hovering disarray, there was an elegant formality in Angela Thornton's demeanour which made Phyllida decide against using her first name again. "I have no family." She watched for empathic reaction to what for most people would be sad news, and after another hesitant moment it appeared.

"Oh ... I'm so sorry, Mrs ... Oh, dear, I've forgotten your name. The way I've started to forget everything." Now, for a moment, there was the unambiguous reaction of panic, and the eyes sought reassurance.

Phyllida put out a hand, and after a reflex twitch the hand on the arm of Mrs Thornton's chair lay motionless beneath it. "I'm Mrs Moon; Phyllida Moon. No husband now, but believe me, that's not a cause for sorrow." Phyllida offered her *alter ego*'s manufactured smile. Warily. Husbands might be a sore point for Mrs Thornton too, or, more likely, a point of sorrow.

The face cleared to full understanding in the moment it grew sad, and for the first time since Phyllida had sat down Angela Thornton looked to be in total touch. "Perhaps you're lucky, Mrs Moon. I lost my husband three years ago, and I still miss him dreadfully. We did everything together. And if he'd been here I wouldn't have to have..." The voice, which had this time been strong and unhesitant, tailed off, and Phyllida thought she saw a mingling of fear and indignation in the eyes before, in an unnerving instant, they turned inward again and Mrs Thornton swung round to face the room. "You're all in it!" she yelled. "Every sodding one of you!"

"Mother! Mother!"

A tall, elegant woman a generation behind Mrs Thornton was crossing the room towards her, arms outstretched and smiling indulgently. As she reached the window her eyes were on Phyllida.

"I'm so very sorry. I'm afraid my mother has – bad moments." The woman had lowered her voice, which rose again as she turned her gaze on to Mrs Thornton. "Mother, what's the matter?" Affection, laced with impatience. "Are you upsetting people again?"

"She's not upsetting me, I promise you," Phyllida said swiftly. "We've been having a very nice chat."

"Liar! Both of you! Filthy liars!"

"Come on, now, Mrs Thornton, that's not a nice thing to say about your daughter and Mrs Moon. And you know it isn't true."

Debbie had been sitting in an armchair on the far side of the room, laughing and talking with one of the residents, but now she was beside them, leaning cajolingly over Mrs Thornton and putting a tentative hand on her shoulder while she smiled a vicarious apology to the other two women.

Mrs Thornton made a move to shake the hand off, then abruptly relaxed and looked up at Debbie with a radiant smile. *"You're* nice. I like *you."*

Phyllida heard the daughter's sharp indrawn breath as Mrs Thornton turned a venomous gaze from her to Phyllida.

"We're all nice," Debbie said, venturing now to squeeze the shoulder. "When we behave ourselves."

So this young girl, who Phyllida had already decided was in the right job, had started to treat Angela Thornton as if she was in her second childhood, on the incentive of a few short bouts of dementia. Phyllida could understand it: once the disease was manifest it could only get worse. Yet Debbie's attitude, which appeared to be the attitude too of Mrs Thornton's daughter, could surely only help to speed up Mrs Thornton's descent.

The most vicious of vicious circles, but one Phyllida could see only a saint escaping.

Well, she would do her best in the next few days to be as saintly as possible, for Angela Thornton's sake as well as the progress of her own mission.

"I'm sorry..." Debbie's reproof had restored the bewilderment. Or it had recurred naturally? Phyllida was pleased to recall something she had just read about the loss of mind: all changes, once a patient is on the slippery slope, come from inside the disappearing brain, which is beyond outside influence. But at what stage does a sufferer slip beyond that influence? Phyllida found herself unhappily suspecting that Mrs Thornton, the major part of whose life was still lived free of those sudden bouts of fury, had not yet reached immunity to the un-intended cruelty of the people who would decide what was to be done with her.

"Look," she said, getting to her feet. "Please have this chair, Mrs ... ?"

"Turner. Emma Turner. Well, if you don't—"

"I want to go to the lavatory." Mrs Thornton was also rising. "So you might as well stay and talk to Emma, Mrs Moon, until I get back."

Phyllida subsided with a nod and a smile, and Angela Thornton turned to face Debbie, who was holding out an arm. "Thank you, Debbie. But I can manage. I'm only here because Emma and the family are going away and she doesn't want to worry about me. I live in a granny flat attached to her house, you see, and she's afraid I might fall, or have a stroke." The voice was still mild, but Phyllida saw the indignation flash again across the eyes. "I thought you were going today, Emma."

"Not for a couple of days yet. I've been tearing round like a mad thing. We're going to Canada, you see," she said to Phyllida. "My husband and I and our two boys."

"Very nice," Mrs Thornton commented. "Now, if you'll excuse me a moment..."

"Let her go," Mrs Turner murmured to Debbie, as her mother began to make her way slowly towards the door. "I'd like a word. Is it getting worse? More frequent? More – violent?"

Phyllida again made a move to get to her

105

feet, and this time it was Mrs Turner who told her to stay put.

"I don't think so," Debbie said. "And there's never any physical violence. Perhaps her language is getting a bit – well – stronger. You'd wonder how such a lady even knows some of the words she says, but this is something that happens to the – well – the poshest of people."

"Has she always wanted to swear?" Emma Turner demanded rhetorically. "If she has, she's been wonderfully self-controlled; I've never heard anything worse than a 'damn'."

"It happens," Debbie said. "But nobody, no doctor, seems to know why. They just know it's a sign of deteriorating ... I'm sorry, Mrs Turner."

"Don't be. I'd rather know the truth, so that we can decide ... I'm asking Dr Hartley if I can keep her leaving date open until we get back in a couple of weeks' time. It'll give us all a chance to see how quickly things change, if they do. It came on very suddenly a couple of months ago, so I suppose it could get worse while we're away."

"I'm afraid it could. But as you said, Mrs Turner, you want peace of mind while you're away, and you know we'll make your mother's stay here as pleasant for her as we possibly can. Now, you go off and enjoy yourselves!"

"Thank you. We'll do our best, but I don't somehow think we'll manage too well ... I'll have half an hour or so with my mother now, take her down the garden. Debbie, would you like to see if she's all right?"

"Surely." With one of her cheerfully reassuring smiles Debbie whirled off, and Mrs Turner sank down with a sigh into the chair her mother had occupied. "It's so sad," she said to Phyllida, her eyes suddenly glittering and her exquisite lips turning down at the corners, "and I haven't begun to get used to it."

It could be that Mrs Thornton's daughter had been displaying a stiff upper lip rather than coldness of heart. Unless, like Phyllida, she was an actress and–

Stop it! That way paranoia *did* lie, playing with the idea that relatives might be in cahoots with doctors.

And Mrs Turner was wiping away real tears. "I'm so sorry," she said. "I didn't want the nurse to see ... I didn't want you, or any-one else, to see, either." When she smiled, as she did now, her lovely face was even lovelier. "I'm afraid I'm not going to be able to cope, if things get worse. As they will. If she stays in the flat I'll never have a moment's peace. And if she moves in with us, none of us will and it won't be fair on the children. So what do I do?"

"Go to Canada. Talk to people there, get as many ideas as possible, but decide for yourselves. And don't think about it all the time; you obviously need a total break." Phyllida realised, with a shiver of dismay, that it was she herself who was speaking. "You're happy about the nursing and medical care here?" Mrs Moon asked, hastily summoned. "I'm just convalescing, so my main consideration was the five-star hotel aspect."

"Stansfield Manor has a good reputation in that area as well. Mother could stay here, I suppose."

"Rather costly, in the long term?"

"Yes." Emma Turner rolled her eyes ceilingwards. "But we can just about find the money. Damn!" She was in tears again, more copiously, and as she blew her nose Phyllida saw her sob. "I'm not used to it yet," Mrs Turner repeated in a choked voice. "And I don't really think I should be going away."

"You'll cope better when you come back. And while you're away you'll know your mother's being well looked after." *That is, if she isn't being done to death.* Phyllida was shocked to find herself having to turn a sudden onset of hysterical laughter into a cough.

"Perhaps you're right. Thanks. You've made me feel better." Mrs Turner looked over her shoulder, then got to her feet. "Here she is."

Mrs Thornton came smiling across the room with Debbie beside her, and put out a hand to her daughter. "I do hope you all have a lovely holiday, darling."

Phyllida thought there was another sob as Emma Turner thanked her. "Would you like a walk in the garden, Mummy?"

"Oh, yes, darling. That would be lovely!"

Debbie went back to the resident she had been talking to when Mrs Thornton had started shouting, but before she had time to settle herself in the chair beside him she was back on her feet and flying out to the hall as the shouting and swearing began again, louder now, and more angry.

Nine

For a while, then, my main problem was to keep the family at bay. I say my main problem, because Peggy's creeping disease went into remission and foolishly, in the face of all I knew, I found myself growing less and less wary in her company – even, for short spells of time, forgetting what lay inescapably ahead, so that the remembering each time was like the initial blow renewed. The family, who saw her only intermittently – and as rarely as I could contrive – and who had never seen her less than herself, were inevitably less impressed by the improvement I reported. I had some difficulty persuading them not to raise the accustomed total of their visits and their invitations and, when we did meet, to continue to treat their sister in their lifelong way, which was to talk at her with their plans and their views. Peggy was a wonderful listener, which had always encouraged her naturally egotistical siblings to expand on their favourite subject:

themselves. This, now, I was grateful for, and even at that dreadful time I saw the irony in my fear that it would be diminished by the new rudimentary empathy they had developed towards her, which I was terrified she would become aware of and be alarmed by.

So I did my best to be at her side when she visited, or was visited by, any of them – not easy in a busy working life. I dreaded coming home and finding her closeted with one or more of them, which of course I too often did, and my heart ached to see the look of slightly alarmed perplexity I had first seen when they had surrounded her the morning after her telephone call to Robert.

"The family seem awfully attentive all of a sudden, Eric. I find myself wondering if they know something about me I don't know about myself. But I know that's nonsense, of course, because I haven't been ill for years and I can't remember when I last saw my doctor."

"I suspect they're realising your worth as they get older, darling." I remember my heart felt so squeezed with love and sorrow I had to struggle to bring my words out lightly. And every time I deceived her I disgusted myself. "Realising that there's one of you who thinks more about the others than about herself."

I was desperately relieved to hear her laugh. "That doesn't sound very likely, Eric." It was unusual for her not to upbraid me gently for being less than complimentary about her brothers and sisters, and I took this as a measure of her anxiety about the change in their behaviour.

After that I called a meeting of them all, minus Peggy, at Pamela's bungalow, and read them a form of riot act. More in sorrow than in anger, and it did slightly tone them down. Life for a time became easier, and even when I found one of them with Peggy when I got home, their departure ceased to be followed by more baffled comments from her on their changed behaviour.

Within a few months, of course, the question of their behaviour towards my wife had become academic. But the episodes of fear and bewilderment came intermittently, still, so that for a time I managed to keep from them the knowledge that the deterioration was once more visibly proceeding.

It resumed one Saturday when the two of us had gone out for lunch. A lovely sunny day in late March, with a rollicking breeze and daffodils along the roadside verges and in the front gardens as prolific as the ones that inspired Wordsworth, so that whenever

I have seen them since they have brought me more pain than pleasure.

I remember I'd asked Peggy where she would like to go and she'd chosen our favourite hostelry, an old house converted to a hotel and restaurant that has a pretty garden to look out on and serves delicious bar snacks. The temporarily restored Peggy was able to cook our main meals in the evening, so that when we went out for lunch we had reverted to our usual lunchtime fare of prawn or smoked salmon sandwiches.

We were early, and the lounge bar was empty. There was nothing to choose between the tables in the big window looking on to the garden, and we settled ourselves at one without comment, it seemed by mutual consent. But after a few moments I saw that Peggy was looking uneasy – saw it even at that stage with a pang of alarm, because it is not one of her usual expressions, her face in repose is invariably serene – and I asked her if anything was the matter.

"Not really," she said, her brows drawn down as she looked from side to side. "But I think we'd be better ... Eric, that table over there" – she nodded towards it – "would be nicer, I think. Let's move!"

The table she had indicated was the mirror image of the one where we were already sitting, in the other corner of the big window, and there was nothing whatever to choose between them. I think I knew then what was happening, but I blocked the knowledge from my conscious mind as I told her all right, if she preferred the look of it, we'd move there.

So we did, but almost immediately after we'd sat down the look of perplexity was back, and as I studied the terrible familiarity of her suddenly unfamiliar face I knew that that moment, beyond the others I had already lived through, was in fact the worst moment of my life.

"Eric ... It's cramped here, compared to that table in the centre of the window. I'm sure we'd be better there." This time she got to her feet without searching my face for a response, and made her way to the next table but one.

That wasn't the end of it, of course. We moved twice more, and I remember reproving myself for being glad the barman was temporarily absent and that no one was witnessing our travels. He reappeared just as we were settling down for the fourth time, and came promptly across on my signal. Peggy was unable to say what she would like to drink so I ordered her a tomato juice, and when the waiter brought the menu and she was unable to say what she wanted to eat, I ordered her what I ordered for myself.

She ate it hesitantly, shifting it about her plate, on which her eyes were fixed in the intervals between the periods of staring out of the window. When I said her name and asked her to talk to me, trying to sound teasing, she gave me no more than a sidelong glance before turning her eyes back either to the barely eaten food or the view through the window. When I made a comment she answered with a grunt, and when I asked a question she said "Yes" or "I don't know", or simply gave a brief smile before looking away again.

When we got back into the car things changed yet again: she began to question my judgement of the road, cowering down in her seat when I passed cars parked on the near side and hissing at me that this or that was coming, or that we were approaching a junction. I remember the fresh disgust I felt at myself, because in the midst of my anguish and compassion it made me angry and I had to bite on a series of acid rejoinders and keep telling myself, *This is not Peggy!* By the time she died, those words had become my mantra.

When I'd parked in front of the house she didn't spring out of the car in her usual lithe way. She stayed in her seat staring through the windscreen, so that when I went round and opened her door I was astonished – and anguished in a different way – to see her looking at me with her old understanding.

And the new perplexity. "Eric," she said, putting out her hand. "I don't think I'm feeling terribly well. In fact, I think I'll lie down. D'you mind, darling? It's just a bit of a headache."

"If you've got a headache I think it's a good idea. Try to go to sleep, and I'll bring up some tea later and we'll have it in the bedroom." I remember I had to bite my tongue again, because I suddenly wanted to tell her how much I loved her, and I reckoned the declaration might be too emotionally charged for her as she was at that moment, perched on the cusp between the light and the dark.

"That would be lovely, darling." She sprang out of the car then, her face clearing, and we walked upstairs together. I prepared the bed while she took off her shoes and jacket – without prompting – and then she got under the duvet and turned on her side with a smile. So I left her and went downstairs. I remember my legs felt like lead and I had to make an effort to lower them from step to step.

When I went back into the bedroom a couple of hours later my hands were trembling so much the crockery on the tray I was carrying was clinking away, and as I crossed the room Peggy yawned and sat up, smiling a mild reproach I recognised with agonised joy.

"You spoil me, Eric! Everyone seems to be spoiling me these days. Well, I'll just enjoy it."

"That's the ticket." Old bits of cliché were coming to the top of my mind, like bits of wrapping paper, to ease the impact of our exchanges. It seems strange, looking back now: the amount of time Peggy had been out of herself had been so minimal, but it was as if the future as well as the past had taken place and I had equally clear sight both backwards and forwards.

The rest of the day was all right, and I think the next couple of weeks, but then something new began: a deterioration in the abilities and performance of my "real" Peggy. It started when she was reading one evening, and I was growing uneasy because ten minutes had gone by and she hadn't turned a page. This had happened in the old days sometimes because she had fallen asleep, but when I looked at her now I saw that her eyes were wide open and staring down at the page.

"The book any good, darling?"

Deception again! But how could I avoid it?

I had to ask the question twice before she responded by raising her head and looking at me. Without seeing me, for a few seconds, but then with her old intimate smile.

"It's a bit boring, actually. One of those books that when you've put it down you have to recap when you pick it up again to remind yourself who's who."

"I know what you mean." But I didn't know whether she was telling me the truth, or covering up for herself, still heartbreakingly aware that she had something to hide.

The next time it was totally different, and even more terrifying.

Casually, one Sunday afternoon when we were sitting together by the open patio doors, she asked me a question.

"Have you heard from Mother?"

My mother had died before I met Peggy, and she and her siblings had adored their own, so there was no ambiguity about whom she was referring to.

But Peggy's mother, too, was dead.

Like the daughter about whose whereabouts she had asked me and Robert.

Oh, that succession of the worst moments of my life! They came thicker and faster.

"Not lately," I remember I replied. I hadn't thought in advance what I might say, because I hadn't envisaged that particular question. But I had become a veteran of her descent to the extent that my reflexes, this time, did not offer her the truth. "Have you?"

"No..." The look of perplexity, deeper and more alarmed than I had so far seen it. "She isn't well, you know."

"I know she's been ill." I just opened my mouth and let words come as they would. "But I thought ... she was better."

"Oh, no. No. Not at all. You know that, Eric." It was a reproach.

"Sorry, darling, yes."

I remember wondering if I should ring Robert, and hoping desperately there would be nothing further to turn speculation into necessity.

And that day there wasn't. It was a couple of days later that I permanently lost contact, that the Peggy I had known and loved for more than twenty-five years disappeared for ever.

Ten

John Bright drove Phyllida to the Agency in the late afternoon a couple of days later and dropped her outside, still without having asked any questions beyond those concerning her convalescence and how she had found Stansfield Manor. He was a plump, cheerful man with an easy manner and Phyllida liked him as well as his discretion, for which she thanked him as he drew up.

"If I wasn't discreet I wouldn't be in your confidence at all, and you wouldn't be using my hotel. I wouldn't like that, Phyllida, and neither would my staff – we enjoy our secret knowledge that we're in the midst of mysteries."

"I couldn't cope with them without you all."

"I'm sure you could, but we're glad you'd rather not. Give me a ring when you're ready to go back."

"I can call a taxi."

"That would make me cross."

"All right, John. Thanks. We'll meet in the hotel car park, though, where you could have dropped me now. I've managed a circuit of the Manor garden."

But Phyllida didn't attempt her usual ascent of the curved shallow stairs; she rode up in the lift. The staff of the Agency had, of course, seen her arrival from the windows, and Jenny was ready with tea and biscuits. Steve was there too, and after smiling indulgently at their studiedly casual faces, Peter invited the young ones to join him and Phyllida in his office.

"I'm afraid there's only one thing so far I can tell you with certainty," Phyllida began, when they were settled in their usual places, she facing Peter across his desk and Jenny and Steve flanking her at either edge. Steve, who hated to give up trying to do anything he saw as a goal, however small, had at first attempted to stay on his feet and lean in casual fashion against the desk, but as usual had failed to feel casual in that position and had pulled up a chair. "The Manor is very well run on the hotel side. It appears to be well run on the nursing side too, and we've got a classic subject lined up, which *pace* Mr Kendrick I wish we hadn't. A Mrs Angela Thornton is on her way over the edge, and her daughter's off to Canada today for a couple of weeks, at the end of which time Mrs Thornton is due to go home." She and Peter stared at one another in silence, and Phyllida heard indrawn breaths from Steve and Jenny. "I should say that eighty per cent of the time Mrs Thornton is a nice, gentle, increasingly frightened lady at whose demise, if the Chief Superintendent is right, I could be a bystander. I feel horribly helpless, Peter. If I was playing crazy I could be found in all sorts of unauthorised places without causing alarm, but as it is I have to be so careful."

"By God you do. And if you were playing crazy they might prefer you to Mrs Thornton."

"*Don't!*"

"He's only joking, Jenny." But Phyllida wasn't amused, either, and gave the boss a severe look as she resumed. "I did find out from Debbie this morning that there are a couple of other residents with early mental problems, and she pointed them out to me: a man and a woman who are quietly confused, but make no public displays like Mrs Thornton's. What she said yesterday about the Alzheimer's residents who died is the most significant thing I've heard so far. 'They hadn't been like that for long and they weren't all that far gone.'" She would never, in the farthest future, have any difficulty recalling those words. "I asked questions about the history of the Manor, with special reference to its recent fate – it was easy enough to ask the receptionist for whatever booklets there were, and then chat on from there – but I don't think I learned anything significant. The Manor was in private hands until fifteen years ago, when it became a girls' school. When that went bust it was empty for a while, and Josie implied that Dr Hartley had acquired it as something of a bargain four or five years ago. She doesn't know what he was doing before he took it over, but I gathered he isn't local. But Maurice Kendrick has to have found all this out already."

"Never mind. You were the one who heard the name Douglas."

"And discovered that it doesn't belong to any members of the staff. If the Chief Superintendent hasn't already done it, can you look into the structure of the management, Peter, in case there's a board, or trustees, or something?"

"He has done it. And tells me the building and grounds belong solely to Dr Hartley, who directed the conversion and made his appointments all on his ownsome."

"That's not very helpful, though it's

interesting in a way. He didn't strike me as a strong enough character to have carried through so much on his own shoulders. But he could be a good delegator."

"Don't they say the most effective bosses are?"

"So perhaps they're right. From what I've seen so far he's got a strong team. And a very efficient one. I was called by my name – Mrs Moon – all along the line, by members of staff I was meeting for the first time. It would be difficult to do anything in the least unorthodox without its being noted."

"But by just observing you've given us something to tell Kendrick." Steve's pale face was briefly pink with excitement. "With an obvious risk of murder over the next couple of weeks he might feel he could insinuate a bodyguard. I might be able to—"

"I haven't observed anything in the least suspicious about the behaviour of any member of staff, Steve," Phyllida responded swiftly. She had seen the rare flash of irritation across Peter's face. "So there's no way Mr Kendrick could do anything, is there, Peter?"

"It'll be up to him when I've reported, but I doubt it. All *we* can do, I should say, is for Phyllida to keep as close to Mrs Thornton as she can without it looking unnatural."

"You could tell someone in authority that you've lost a dear one to the disease, so that you feel a special sympathy for her," Jenny suggested.

"That's a great suggestion, Jenny!" Looking from Peter's approving smile to the scowl on Steve's face, Phyllida too felt a moment of irritation at the reaction of the thin-skinned cockney youth whose ego was even frailer than her own – she, at least, was never fazed by brilliance in others. But the next moment the feeling was subsumed in the sense of pity Steve more habitually awoke in her, which he would so fiercely have resented had he known of it: behind his habitual defensive guise of reluctance, he gave so much of himself to the Agency, the obvious centre of his life. She suspected hopefully, though, that with security in the job he loved he was growing a bit less brittle – now, he had erased the scowl and managed to replace it with a hint of approval of Jenny's suggestion.

"I'll certainly do that," Phyllida continued. "And Mrs Thornton as herself is a charming woman. It shouldn't seem too strange."

Steve asked her why she was smiling.

"I suppose because we've found something specific for me to do." Because the adrenalin was flowing again.

Jenny asked her what it was like sleuthing in her own character.

"I was wary at first, Jenny, I felt sort of naked. But then I discovered I'd become someone else even without a disguise. In the way I was behaving, I mean."

"What *do* you mean?" Jenny pressed eagerly. "Tell us!"

"I didn't try; I'd no idea what would happen. But ... well, Mrs Moon is more extrovert than Miss Moon: she takes the lead in conversation, says things – in a different way from the way I'd say them. It's hard to describe it, but as well as helping me find things out it feels like a sort of protection. And a sort of disguise, I suppose."

"Which you can't take off," Steve reminded her unnecessarily. "Who will you be if you meet the Director in the street this time next year? If he's still at large, that is. He'll recognise you, and think it's Mrs Moon."

"I know." The goose was back. "That's the difference with this new disguise from all the others. But she looks just like me and I'm pretty confident no one will remember her so minutely." She *was* confident, of course, it was common sense, but even though she was openly at the Manor as her convalescent self, Phyllida realised as she spoke that even inside Mrs Moon's invisible protection she was constantly aware of a sense of vulnerability she had never felt before.

"I'd love to be around!" Jenny said. "It'd be much more interesting than seeing you really disguised."

"It *is* interesting. When I find myself responding as – who I really am – if I'm asked about something *I* think is important, then I feel sort of draughty until I can pop back into Mrs Moon."

"You'll have to write a paper one day," Peter said. "Or at least an article for the press. In the far future, of course; I can't have you jeopardising your uniqueness for years and years yet."

"Thanks, but I can start making notes." Which she was going to do, Phyllida decided. She was as intrigued by what had happened as Jenny was. "I wondered if I'd find Mr Kendrick here."

"I think he was tempted," Peter said. "Then decided it would be a bit over the top at this stage. I got the feeling when we last spoke that the lady who alerted him isn't letting him forget her suspicions. I'll ring him when you've gone."

"And mention Douglas?"

"If you agree. He might be able to enlighten us."

"Fine. Now, tell me what's been happening here. I feel I've been away for years." All the more so because the last time she had been in the Agency she had believed that within the next forty-eight hours she would be in a place where the people around her could include Dr Pusey.

Having discovered that without a physical disguise she needed a few solitary, concentrated moments to think herself into her *alter ego*, after being dropped at the entrance to the Manor by John Bright, Phyllida went upstairs with no more delay than it took to tell Josie Durant she had had a nice afternoon. *Not my* alter ego! she corrected herself sharply as she drew a chair up to her bedroom window. *Jack Pusey wouldn't give her a second look!* And she wouldn't have done either, Phyllida thought, ruefully amused, if Mrs Moon hadn't been her own creation.

During the afternoon the weather had slowly deteriorated, and as she watched the last pools of pale blue disappear behind spreading and darkening clouds her view was suddenly patterned by slashes of rain slanting across the centre of her window. The next moment Debbie appeared from the nearest enclave, an elderly lady on either arm and laughing so loudly as she let them dictate the pace of their run towards the house that Phyllida could hear the laugh as well as see it in Debbie's parted lips and thrown-back head.

Fifteen minutes had passed since she had entered her room, and it was time to go downstairs and reveal a softer side to Mrs Moon than had yet been demonstrated. As she stiffened herself mentally for her next entry on stage, Phyllida's body reminded her that it was still convalescent and she glanced wistfully at her white bed before propelling herself resolutely into the corridor, where to her relief the adrenalin took over and her body as well as her mind was ready to be back at work.

At first when she entered the lounge she couldn't see Mrs Thornton, and was irritated by her absurd sense of relief when she spotted her alone at the far end of the room, looking out through the side window. Even if Detective Chief Superintendent Kendrick's wife's cousin's suspicions were justified, Angela Thornton would scarcely have been despatched less than twenty-four hours after her daughter had left her in good physical health.

Sister Anne was talking to someone by the main window and hadn't looked up, but Phyllida went through the motions of looking round the room apparently without intent before making her way across to Mrs Thornton.

"Hello!" she said softly, as she sat slowly down in the empty chair beside her. "May I join you?"

For a moment there was no response from the woman gazing through the window. Phyllida steeled herself for a blaze of anger that would engulf the room ... and maybe – another absurd but ghastly thought was in her mind before she could forbid it entry – hasten Mrs Thornton's end.

"Oh! Please do! I was hoping to talk to you again."

So her short-term memory wasn't yet entirely lost. "That's nice. I was hoping to talk to you again, too. Have you been in the garden today?" There had been no further outbursts since Mrs Turner's departure the day before, to pinpoint her mother's whereabouts.

A slight perplexity, as Mrs Thornton considered. "Yes," she said, her face clearing as she smiled at Phyllida. "This morning, just before lunch. It was fine then; the sun was shining. Emma rang this morning, you know, to say goodbye again."

"That's nice," Mrs Moon repeated. "Have *you* ever made the trip to Canada?"

"Yes!" No hesitation, and the eyes were bright with happy memory. "A long time ago, with my husband. When Emma was at boarding school. I think I'd have liked to go again, with Emma and Frank now, to see my brother for probably the last time, but they said the long journey would be a bit too strenuous for me, and ... and ... I can't remember the other reasons they didn't think it was a good idea, but otherwise they'd have taken me, they said. I'd asked God, but if nothing happens it means he doesn't agree, you see. So I couldn't have gone."

Out of the mouths of babes and mystics ... Phyllida couldn't keep a journal of her own attempted doings, but she could write down the luminous words of a woman who had just confirmed her entry into another dimension.

"No. I see. Will you excuse me a moment, Mrs Thornton, while I make a note in my diary? Something I've just remembered and which I'll forget again if I don't write it down."

"Of course, dear." Mrs Thornton's gaze

was back on the garden, but tranquil and contemplative. "I think Will's my brother," she said, as Phyllida put pen and diary back in her bag. "But then there's a nephew..."

"You'll be able to sort it out when your daughter comes back with lots of photographs."

"Bugger photographs!"

Phyllida had thought she was ready, but the impact of the sudden loud fury was so great she sprang on a reflex to her feet and found she had put a hand on Mrs Thornton's shoulder without wondering whether or not it was a good idea.

Mrs Thornton brushed it off as if it was a fly. "You're all the same!" she shouted. "Every bleeding one of you!"

"Now, Mrs Thornton!" Sister Anne, of course, was with them, leaning down to Mrs Thornton and taking her hand.

"You can sod off!" Mrs Thornton pulled her hand free, put it to her lips as if it was hurting her, then started to cry.

"There, dear, it's all right!"

Phyllida was glad to see Sister Anne's face warm for a moment as she put it close to Mrs Thornton's. "I'm sorry," she said. "We were chatting quite happily, but I suppose I could have started her off."

"She doesn't need a trigger, Mrs Moon.

132

Dear me, you must have had a shock."

"Not really." Phyllida paused for an instant while she slipped back into Mrs Moon. "I had a cousin who was afflicted in the same way. She died, but we'd been close when we were young and I went on spending time with her as she got worse. So in a way I'm used to it, and I always feel a – well, an especial pity for people suffering like she did, and I want to help them, even though I know I can't."

"I always hope they don't know they're suffering." For the second time Phyllida saw a glimpse of feeling in Sister Anne's face, which disappeared into wariness as the Sister turned her gaze back on to Mrs Thornton.

"Not eventually," she agreed. "But Mrs Thornton's still well enough most of the time to be aware that the world's slipping away from her. She's frightened, Sister."

"I know." Now there was sudden fear in Sister Anne's eyes, which she dropped as if to hide it, patting Mrs Thornton's arm without evoking reaction before looking up at Phyllida with her usual lack of expression restored. "And we're all very sorry about it."

If she hadn't spotted those brief glimpses of warmth and fear Phyllida would have suspected Sister Anne of being unaffected by Mrs Thornton's affliction, but now she found herself wondering if the indifference could be a façade. "She's happy to chat still for most of the time." She had dropped her voice to a whisper, even though Mrs Thornton, now silent and immobile, was staring down the garden again with the long, inward look that told her she would not hear what was said. "And I'm happy to chat with her; it feels a bit like doing something more for my cousin, in an odd way, if that makes any sense."

"Of course it does." Whatever her real reaction, there was nothing else Sister Anne could have said.

"So I won't be upsetting her, you don't think? I wouldn't like to make life more difficult for you and other members of your staff."

"Of course not, Mrs Moon, it would be very good of you. I'm afraid you'll have to be aware all the time, though, that another outburst will come without warning. It could be a bit hard on your nerves, especially as you're convalescent."

"At least *you're* warning me, Sister." Warning her off? "So I'll see how it goes. Not glue myself to her side, of course, but it does seem that she gets left rather severely alone."

"That's a sad result of anti-social illness, I'm afraid. So it will certainly be a kindness on your part to have the occasional chat."

"Good. And I must tell you, Sister," Mrs Moon went on, "how much I'm enjoying your five-star hotel. My room, the food, the way you look after me ... It's wonderful!"

"Thank you." To Phyllida's surprise Sister Anne offered a toothpaste-ad smile, along with another tinkly laugh. "We do our best, and it's always nice to be told that our residents appreciate it."

"How could they not?" Mrs Moon at her most winsome, Phyllida reflected, as she felt the unnatural width of her own smile. "The Manor must be a lovely place to work in."

"When one has time to notice." Now there was a pettish note in Sister Anne's voice.

"It must be distressing to have a patient like Mrs Anderson, one moment quite normal, and the next—"

"It *is* distressing!" Suddenly the wide blue eyes were bright with what Phyllida could only call in her mind a look of outrage. It was gone so quickly she wondered for a moment if she had imagined it but knew she had not, any more than she had imagined the warmth and the fear. "That's why one grows an extra skin."

So it could be true: Sister Anne could have

cultivated the prevailing detachment of her approach to her work which Phyllida had at first seen as her natural reaction, and those seconds of feeling could have broken through it. *Could have, could be* ... There was no way of knowing and however it was, Phyllida thought glumly, it threw no light on an investigation she felt at that moment was likely never to get off the ground.

"And now I think I'll have a walk in your beautiful garden," Mrs Moon resumed enthusiastically as, to Phyllida's relief, her professional reflexes took over. "The sun seems to be on the way back." A good idea, she supposed, to demonstrate without delay that Mrs Moon's concern for Mrs Thornton was only one aspect of her sojourn at the Manor.

"You'll be all right on your own? You still look a little frail, Mrs Moon."

"I'm tougher than I appear, Sister. I'll be fine."

"If you're sure, then."

"I'm sure." Sister Anne was clearly poised to move on, so Phyllida accompanied her as far as the old man who was trying to attract her attention, then carried on out to the terrace to resume the battle, the moment she was alone, against the bleak sense of inevitable failure she had never felt before during the course of an investigation, however unpromising.

It had to be her state of health, Phyllida urged herself: post anaesthetic, post surgery, post (if only!) her personal disappointment. For a few moments she would stop driving herself, forget work, be aware only of being in a beautiful garden on a restored summer evening. She still had time in which to look and listen.

The decision worked for the few moments it took her to reach the first enclave on the left of the descent of lawn, still an all-over gold in the sun's low western rays. By the time she entered it she had identified a few of her favourite herbaceous blooms, confirmed her decision that, for a small garden like her own, shrubby growths were both easier and more attractive, and begun to feel slightly more serene.

Until she turned into the enclave and discovered the Director on the farthest of the elegant wrought-iron seats, engaged in such apparently distressing conversation with the boyishly attractive woman sitting beside him that the adrenalin began pumping and with one heartbeat she had regained the excitement of the chase.

Eleven

It was in the night that I lost her finally.

We had gone up to bed together as usual one Saturday evening in June, after a day in which despite my knowledge and my fears I had been intermittently happy. Peggy had appeared happy all the time, no perplexity throughout the day in her dear smiling, teasing face. I remember, still with anguish, how I made myself say in my head, *This is happening now! This is real! This is once and for all!* as I gazed at her. That truth still comforts me, but the bleakness is always waiting, and when it pounces it is still a body blow...

I always tended to wake first, and I did so the next morning. Peggy was lying curled up on her side, facing away from me, so still and peaceful that I slid out of bed carefully and went barefoot to the bathroom. When I came back she was as I had left her, and I went round the bed to see if she was as deeply asleep as she appeared to be, crouching down in front of her to study her face.

It had the blank look of the sleeper, so I wasn't worried – and was utterly unaware that I was enjoying the last comparatively happy moments of my life – as I gazed at her. It was Sunday, I wasn't due in at work, but it was nine o'clock, my stomach was rumbling, and Peggy always chided me if I didn't ensure she was awake in time to make our tea and toast and be with me at the breakfast table. So I started to stroke her hair, gently, then moved my hand down the side of her face.

When it reached her neck her own hand shot up from under the bedclothes and seized it tightly. At the same time her eyes snapped open and stared at me with a blankness that slowly cleared to what I defined as an uncertainty, a doubt as to what she should do.

And that was what it was, and how from that moment onwards it remained.

She had started to mumble softly, and it took me a few moments, bending very close to her, to make out words like, "Shall I ... I don't know ... Do you think..." I can't remember them precisely because they were so imprecise. But their message was clear: they were the questions of someone who had awakened without a sense of identity, and thence of purpose.

As she lay mumbling there, her face a mask of worry and indecision, I rang Robert. It was the only time since I became part of his monstrous family that I have looked to any member of it other than Peggy for comfort, but at that moment I needed someone – perhaps anyone – to take away the terrible awareness of being alone while still in the company of the companion of my life.

"Yes?"

"It's happened." I remember I answered him as abruptly as his sleepy, snappy monosyllable had answered me. "She's awake, but she isn't with me. This is different, Robert. You'd better come over."

"Right away. You OK, Eric?" I'd been overtaken by a sudden sob as I said the last couple of words.

"Of course not. I need you, Robert." I'd never said anything like that to any member of Peggy's family before, either.

"I'm on my way."

It was terrible going back to Peggy's side of the bed. I hadn't said anything at work up till then about her condition, and neither, I knew, had any of the family. I remember worrying for a moment – the sort of irrelevance I was to learn sometimes takes over, when one has an all-consuming desperate worry, like a temporary stony resting place – that people outside the family would now have to be informed of what had happened to my wife.

She was as I had left her, still muttering broken-off phrases, still with that terrible forlorn-cum-panicky look of a lost child.

I had no idea what to expect, but she didn't resist me as I pulled her gently to a sitting position, raised the pillows, and laid her back against them.

"It's all right, Peggy darling, it's all right. You've just had a nasty dream."

If only! Yet for a mad moment I found myself hoping I was right, and that the uncertainty in her eyes would clear to her usual radiant smile.

It didn't, of course, and she stared at me as if she had never seen me in her life before.

"Where am I?" It was her first complete sentence. She spoke it clearly and like an idiot I rejoiced. How comparative are our expectations!

"You're at home, darling. And still in bed at ten past nine because it's Sunday. So I can make the breakfast and bring it upstairs. You'd like that, wouldn't you?"

I didn't know it then, but I had set the standard I was to maintain to the end of her life. I never talked to her like she was less than the self she had lost, but as if that self was still a child.

A child who, this second time, would never grow up. Oh, Peggy!

"Breakfast ... Yes..."

"I'll be just a moment, darling. Have another snooze if you like, or here's your book."

Before going to sleep she had been reading a layman's guide to philosophy, and I laid it on the sheet in front of her. Keeping up appearances. Because, at least while I was still in shock, I needed to. Peggy picked it up and started riffling the pages, her anxiety deepening so that after a few seconds I took it away from her. She didn't notice.

Robert arrived while I was down in the kitchen – on his own, thank heaven; I couldn't have coped with any more of them so soon. I was amazed that for the second time he took me in his arms and I was comforted, experiencing him, for the first time, as a part of Peggy that was still itself.

"I love her so, Robert." I hadn't known I was going to say that. And I didn't know, when I started to write this story of her descent, that I would have such total recall, especially as I had banished these details from my conscious mind. It's as if my subconscious has been their protection, like green baize around silver, and they're emerging now as bright as when I wrapped them away.

It's a terrible experience, but it would be worse if I were struggling to bring it all back, and then whatever came I found had tarnished.

Knowing something in theory is not like experiencing it in practice, and Robert, of course, was in no way prepared for what I showed him upstairs. Peggy was lying back just as I had left her, her eyes staring into space, and it took a moment for her to turn her head in response to his urgent pleas. He had dropped immediately to his knees beside her and their faces were close as he looked at her beseechingly, tears running down his cheeks. That was yet another first for me: the only time I've ever been remotely sorry for a member of Peggy's family.

Peggy looked back at him in puzzlement, and then her face broke into a delighted smile – a child's smile – and she put a hand up to his face.

"You're nice!" she pronounced. "I like you!"

Robert took her head between his hands,

kissed the top of it, then got to his feet and turned to face me. "Poor Eric!" he said, when he had blown his nose and wiped his eyes, and I was as grateful for those words as I have ever been for anything. He knew where the worst anguish lay, and would lie. Unlike his siblings, who saw Peggy's disappearance, that day and ever after, principally in terms of its impact on their entity – the Family.

But they had to be brought in. I remember muttering it.

"Yes, but you can leave it to me if you prefer. Would you like me to contact them?"

"Yes, please, Robert."

I discovered something else at that moment. A tragedy that destroys one's life neutralises lesser upsets: the imminent descent of Peggy's other siblings was suddenly irrelevant in the light of my loss of her.

Robert sat down on my side of the bed, rang George, got Mona, told her what had happened, and asked her or George to contact the others. I remember him covering the receiver as he turned to ask me what time they should come, and that I shrugged and said they could come whenever they pleased. The pain at that moment was our both realising, without putting it into words, that there was no need to whisper the terrible news, that even if Peggy's ears took it in her mind would fail to make sense of it.

At least – and this was the only point of warmth in the icy world I had that morning entered – there was no way now that any of us, or anyone else in the world, could possibly hurt her. She was out of reach.

Twelve

It was the way it had been the first time Phyllida had encountered Dr Hartley tête-à-tête in the garden: he agitated, his female companion apparently unruffled. Silent-footed on the grass and coming to a halt just short of the sunshaft, Phyllida had time to register the calm face of the woman beside him as well as the gleam of sweat on the Director's pallid temple and the anxious distortion of his mouth.

And to hear what he was saying.

"... so we've got to make Jor – we've got to make Douglas realise how essential it is for him to ... Ah! Mrs Moon!"

In an instant the only evidence remaining of the Director's disarray was the sweat now beginning to run down his cheek, so that as he got to his feet, smiling his tight professional smile, he took out a handkerchief and discreetly mopped it away.

The woman remained sitting as Phyllida advanced towards them, registering no reaction to the inadvertent intrusion. She was not in her first youth, but her short dark hair showed off a long graceful neck, and she had noticeable facial bones and what looked like a long thin body.

"Mrs Moon!" Dr Hartley repeated. "I don't think you've yet met Dr Shaw, who shares the care of our residents with Dr Clifford. Mrs Moon is recovering from the loss of her gall bladder, Doctor."

"Mrs Moon."

As she repeated the name Dr Shaw rose slowly to her feet, exceeding Phyllida's estimate of her physique as she uncoiled to half a head taller than Phyllida's own above-average height.

"Dr Shaw."

"We'd ask you to join us in contemplation of a beautiful evening," Dr Shaw said, "if business didn't call us back indoors." The voice was a low, attractive drawl.

"Not that we have been idling here!" Another corrective from the Director, who Phyllida suspected had just administered one to himself. "In the summer we are sometimes tempted to discuss the running of the Manor in the garden." Phyllida noted how carefully Dr Shaw watched Dr Hartley as he spoke. "These enclaves seem made for the exchange of ideas."

"Perhaps they were," Phyllida suggested.

"They look like they were an original feature of the garden. Am I right?"

"Yes!" Enthused, the Director seemed suddenly more spontaneous and less predictable than Phyllida had hitherto defined him. "The garden and the house were designed together. I have the original deeds, and all the enclaves are there."

"It's a beautiful place. In a beautiful part of the countryside. Do you live nearby, Dr Shaw?"

"Oh, yes. Just around the corner. It's very convenient." The half-smile was somehow private, and was accompanied by a glance at the Director in which Phyllida thought she saw a trace of amusement.

Dr Hartley was clearly not amused, and the enthusiasm abruptly left his face as he started walking towards the lawn, not looking back to see if Dr Shaw was following him.

More nuances, Phyllida reflected ruefully, the only content so far of the report she was preparing in her head.

Except for the reiteration of the name Douglas, which belonged to a man with another name that was not to be uttered. A name under which, perhaps, he had committed some medical sin and been struck off the register? Whatever had happened, it

148

shouldn't be beyond her powers to put the names to their owner, although the discovery might have to wait upon her second incarnation at the Manor.

"I'll sit here for a while, I think," she said to Dr Shaw, as they stood side by side regarding the Director's retreating back. "It's still warm and the sun's bang on the seat."

"Sorry I can't sit with you."

Phyllida suspected approval in the lazy gaze, and mentally accorded her temporary persona the credit. Mrs Moon was so far doing her proud. She even emboldened her an hour later, in a corner of the lounge, to ask Debbie – swooped temporarily to rest on the window seat between her and an intermittently smiling Mrs Thornton – if Drs Clifford and Shaw got on with one another. She asked it idly, but with what felt like a slightly mischievous smile.

"I don't think they meet all that often." Debbie hadn't paused to consider, and Phyllida chalked up one more small disappointment. "But I haven't seen or heard that they don't get on when they do."

"Which you obviously would, in a closed community like this. No professional rivalry, then."

"Well, no. They have priority on-call

times, and if we need a doctor and the one on duty isn't available, we call the other. It works fine."

That was how it would appear to work, Phyllida conceded wearily, if the two doctors were part of a conspiracy, and how it could work in fact if one or neither of them was. "Everything works fine at Stansfield Manor. I wonder any of your residents ever want to leave."

"They often don't." Debbie's face flushed with the pride she seemed to feel as a reflex every time the Manor received a compliment. "'Cept for those who don't know the time of day, or feel their families have imprisoned them here against their will. If you felt like *that*, you'd even want to get away from Buckingham Palace, wouldn't you?"

"I suppose you would, Debbie. What's your other name, by the way?" One of the Manor's brochures had given Phyllida the negative information that neither the Director, the Senior Sister, Sister Anne, Dr Clifford or Dr Shaw possessed "Douglas" or a name beginning "Jor" among their recorded names; but Debbie, her two juniors and the kitchen staff were nowhere listed.

"Kitchen." Debbie pulled a face. "Just as well I don't work there; I'd never hear the end of it."

"I can imagine! Are you really Deborah?"

"Yep. And I'd made up my mind when I left school I'd make people call me by the full name, but of course they don't."

"Never mind; it seems to be the fate of most Deborahs to be called Debbie. A pity, though, because it's a pretty name."

"So is yours, Mrs Moon. Do *you* manage to get the whole works?"

"I – yes. Yes, I do." Now she thought about it, the only person who had ever tried to call her Phyl had been a cheeky stage hand, years ago in Whitby. She'd probably remembered it just because it was a one-off. But what kind of a person was it, Phyllida suddenly wondered on a wave of self-dissatisfaction, who had never had a three-syllable name shortened? Someone, it had to be, without the common touch.

"I think that's wonderful. Shows – well, a sort of dignity."

Deborah's character-reading only reinforced Phyllida's new-born unease, particularly as her own estimation of Mrs Moon had been that she might be somewhat lacking in that quality. What world did she live in?

"Heavens, Debbie! You don't think of *me* as dignified, do you?"

Debbie had flushed, but she appeared to

be thinking up a reasoned reply. "In a way," she came out with, after a moment's pause. "Perhaps the word's 'quality'; I'm not sure. You're awfully easy to talk to and feel relaxed with, but I'm aware all the time of that ... well, quality, dignity, I don't know what to call it. Oh, Lord, I'm sorry, Mrs Moon, I'm getting all tied up!"

"Not at all, Debbie; you've just paid me a compliment." Most of which, Phyllida wistfully conceded, should go to her assumed persona, some of whose reactions she should perhaps think about retaining in her own ... The contrast between her fears about Mrs Moon seeming brash and the reality of the character's impact was so bizarrely wide she was suddenly having to suppress a strong desire to laugh at herself, the only form of navel-gazing with which she was comfortable. "Now, let's talk about something more interesting. How's Mrs Thornton been this last couple of hours? I'd only just joined her when you came over."

"And I've only just come on. But according to Sister Anne's notes she's been fine all afternoon. That's right, isn't it, dear? You've enjoyed this afternoon?"

Debbie had raised her voice and bent towards Mrs Thornton, whose vague smile slowly focused on her face.

"What ... ? I'm sorry, I'm not quite..."

"That's all right, Mrs Thornton, we're just nattering away here."

"You're in the right job," Phyllida said quietly, as Mrs Thornton's face cleared and she made a little nestling movement against the back of her chair. "I like to see an expert at work."

"D'you work, Mrs Moon? Gosh, there I go again, but you sort of make me—"

"It's all right, Debbie, I don't mind. I used to be an actress." Phyllida wondered if she would have told Debbie about *A Policeman's Lot* if it hadn't been for the Agency, and decided that she wouldn't. But at the same time she had to admit to a *frisson* of edgy pleasure at revealing something about her real self while on the job, a pleasure she realised with surprise she had already felt once before: after Chief Superintendent Kendrick had rumbled her and she was telling him about the set-up at the Golden Lion.

"Go on! That's great! Have you been on TV?"

"Nothing so grand. Just with a company that travels around and does seasons in local theatres. That's how I came to be in Seaminster; we were playing the Empress last autumn, and when the season was over I decided to stay on here."

"Because you fell in love with the place?" Debbie's flush of pleasure was back, her proprietorial pride appearing to extend to the coast.

"Among other factors, yes."

So what are you doing now? Debbie had done no more than part her lips, but Phyllida heard the query in her head and let her eyes rest gravely for a moment on the girl's until she saw from their reaction that there would be no more questions. Was this what Debbie had meant by "dignity"? If so, Phyllida began to think it could be useful rather than dismaying to possess it, and reminded herself for good measure that someone who could appear so successfully to be a woman of the streets couldn't be too painfully ladylike. She had learned in her work with the Agency, to her abiding amazement, that one of the easiest roles for her to assume was that of the prostitute. Not in effect, of course, and for as little time as possible in a situation where she might actually be propositioned, but the character always evoked the classic reactions of repulsion or attraction from the people she encountered in the role, both male and female.

A sense of mischief was not something

Phyllida had invented for Mrs Moon; she possessed it herself, a saving grace she had sometimes thought, and it always amused her to be aware how well – and how enjoyably – she was playing a woman she could never play in life. Playing it well, perhaps, for that reason, because it was just a plum role, a good piece of theatre. The difficult roles were the ones closest to herself – among which, Phyllida was discovering, perhaps to her disappointment, she was unable to include Mrs Moon...

"Debbie! Can you come and help, please! It's time to start the move into the dining room."

Supper time. Nearly halfway through her stay and so little achieved. Looking round, Phyllida saw that the Howards were in their places to either side of the fireplace, sherries in hand, and that the young careworker who had helped Debbie and Sister Anne at earlier meals was back on duty. The high sun was making supper feel like high tea, but at least it was six o'clock, later by an hour or more than nursing homes usually served their evening meals. Pouring herself some sherry, Phyllida smiled again as she thought of the Watsons' distaste if forced to sit down to the more customary five o'clock repast.

They had, they informed her complainingly at table, had a totally frustrating afternoon. Something to do with a misunderstood invitation from a cousin, who had been expecting them the next day, but Phyllida listened only to the extent of being sure of offering the right kind of monosyllabic interjection during their pauses for dramatic effect. This was necessary because once again all their remarks were directed at her, and Mrs Anderson sat silent, turning her head from time to time to look out of the window, unless Phyllida spoke to her. The progress of the meal was so dull and frustrating that Phyllida had constantly to remind herself that the food was interesting and the fact of her sitting there passively being supplied with it was speeding her return to her usual energetic working life.

The trouble was, she decided, as she took an orange from the overflowing bowl Debbie had just placed in the centre of the table, that without a physical disguise there was so little she could do. In all her work for the Agency up to now, her disguises had given her *entrée* to places she could never have penetrated looking like herself, which was the one enormous disadvantage of the character of Mrs Moon.

Mrs Anderson, too, had taken a piece of

fruit from the bowl. The remaining contents had shifted to fill the gap, and Phyllida found an aesthetic corner of her mind suddenly satisfied by the new arrangement, to the extent that she wanted to paint it. And, more with thoughts of the garden and urged on by Jenny, she had brought her water-colours...

She herself would have hated to work unnecessarily in public, especially indoors, and would have asked if she could take the bowl upstairs to her room, but Mrs Moon had no such inhibitions, and asked Debbie when she appeared with the coffee if the bowl could be carried through to a corner of the big window in the lounge and placed on the window seat, where she would like to paint it against a background of the garden.

Debbie's face lit up. "Of course, Mrs Moon, I'll take it for you. Everyone'll be interested."

Phyllida tried not to cringe. "Could you carry it really carefully, d'you think, Debbie? The fruit's arranged itself just the way I'd like to try and paint it. If you could bring me some water in a glass or jar, that's all I'll need. I promise not to make a mess." And she was promising herself a more interesting evening than she had anticipated, as well as creating the possibility of attracting the attention of a member of the staff other than Debbie.

At each of the meals Phyllida had now eaten in the Manor's dining room her table had finished ahead of the others, and she was at least able to install herself in her chosen corner with no more audience than the fascinated Debbie, there promptly with the bowl and, a few moments later, a large jar of water, which she set down with a flourish on the nearest polished table.

"I should have asked you for a tablecloth of some sort," Phyllida said. "Oh, dear, I'm being an awful nuisance." The prospect of painting – a lifetime's solitary corrective to unhappiness and disappointment – had taken her out of her role, and Phyllida hastily tempered the abject sound of her words with Mrs Moon's feisty smile.

"Course you're not! But these tabletops are specially treated; you can't damage them ... Can I come and look while you're painting?"

"Of course, Debbie, if you have time and can be bothered." Still a little too self-effacing. This was turning out to be one of her most difficult roles. "Now..."

It worked, as it always did. Phyllida turned the fruit to the angle at which it had attracted her, and impressionistically rendered

158

pinky-gold sky, a blur of herbaceous colour and green-gold grass as its surround before beginning to define the still life inside it. She was aware of people being settled around her but, as always when she found a subject that intrigued her, she disappeared into her attempts to capture it, looking up briefly when a human shadow encroached on her paper with the sort of distance-focused, preoccupied smile with which one hopes to be able to avoid admitting recognition of an acquaintance one is about to pass in the street. She was dimly aware that the background murmurs were complimentary, but it was only when a hand descended on her shoulder and a voice actually addressed her that she came back to herself and turned round.

"Not bad, Mrs Moon."

Hand and voice belonged to Dr Clifford, and the fingers of the hand continued their slight individual pressure for a few seconds as he and Phyllida regarded one another.

"Thank you," she said, as the hand was withdrawn. "It's just a hobby, but the way the fruit had arranged itself caught my eye."

"I like it. Sister Caroline! Have a look at this." The tall figure was bent over a man in the other corner of the big window, but it straightened up and came immediately to the summons.

"It's good, Mrs Moon." The voice remained authoritative, but the severity of the Senior Sister's gaze softened as it focused approvingly on Phyllida's picture.

Phyllida herself turned back to look objectively at her effort for the first time, and saw that, even though there was more to be done, she had caught what she had hoped to catch. The thrill of satisfaction, boosted by the netting of two of the bigger of the Manor's fishes, brought the adrenaline flowing and a rare sense of accord with the ebullient Mrs Moon.

"Thank you, Sister. Doctor..."

Following a hard gaze, Dr Clifford nodded and moved away.

"I do some watercolour myself," Sister Caroline said sternly. "A very difficult medium, but satisfying when one manages to bring it off."

"Yes! You work in a constant state of anxiety, don't you? You can correct oil, acrylic, but you can only muddy watercolour. But I still like it best."

"So do I. Particularly out of doors."

"Me too. I'd like to see some of your—"

The rest of Phyllida's polite request was drowned by the sudden shouts coming from a corner of the side window.

"No, I don't want to go to the toilet! You can go and – boil yourself! Stinkpot!"

"Second childhood," Sister Caroline pronounced. "It's well named. They talk about Mummy and Daddy, and offer the sort of verbal abuse children hurl at one another."

Phyllida's painting was forgotten. "You've worked in an EMI home, Sister?"

"Yes." The sudden look of pain in the dark eyes reminded Phyllida for a moment of the unexpected brief transformation of Sister Anne. "Once, for a short time."

The loud, indignant voice was continuing to ring out, and Sister Caroline straightened up, retrieving her customary look of invulnerability. "I must go to Mrs Thornton. Perhaps you would like to see my work at some time."

"I would indeed."

"Thank you. I'm afraid it will have to be at a time of my choosing."

"I have all the time in the world." But if the week looked like running out without a renewed invitation, Phyllida would prompt her fellow artist.

With a brief nod Sister Caroline moved swiftly away, and Phyllida half turned to watch her approach the angry Mrs Thornton, unappeased by Dr Clifford kneeling at her side. Whether it was Sister Caroline's strong will, or whether Mrs Thornton's outburst had run its course, abruptly the shouting ceased and Mrs Thornton began to look from the nurse to the doctor with her usual gentle smile. Phyllida also saw, as she turned back to her work, that the one thing which had run its course that evening for sure was her inspiration. She accepted the situation cheerfully: the painting wasn't finished, but what she had done had secured one particular summer sunset and one particular arrangement of fruit in a bowl and she would be able to complete it without further need of her models.

The weariness of inactivity had been defeated, but although Phyllida slept well her sleep was streaked with letters of the alphabet jerking across her dreaming eye and refusing to coalesce into words. "Jorlas" and "Dougdan" were the closest she could get, and it was a relief to wake in the early morning and lie visionless, watching the steady return of the sun through her thin curtains and realising, with surprise and disapproval, that she was aware of the precise spot on her shoulder where Dr Clifford's hand had rested.

Thirteen

In oh! such a short time, the new regime seemed to have been in existence for ever, and my life with my dear lost Peggy a long-gone dream of paradise.

At least, with my loss of her, I had lost the cruelty of hope, which despite my awareness of the inevitable had surged so foolishly whenever she had achieved the continuity of a day or two as her true self.

It really was a new regime: that one night had rendered her incapable of doing anything for herself, let alone for me and for our home, and she could no longer be left alone. My work took me away from the house for long, irregular hours, but we already had a cleaner, and at least there was the money to recruit a couple of good cook-cum-nurses, turn and turn about. At night I wanted her to myself.

Another "at least" was that for most of the time she seemed to be contented, although there were sudden descents into anxiety and

– mercifully rarely – panic and terror, which took long caresses with murmurs of encouragement to dispel. During my working day, even in the midst of offering encouragement and reassurance to other people, I would find myself shuddering inwardly at the thought of Peggy, suddenly overcome, having only a paid nurse to turn to.

Or Mona. The Family, of course, were eager to take their part in caring for her, and there was no way I could refuse them. Mona, the one I feared most next to Pamela, did only voluntary part-time work (which, given the opportunity, she would talk about full time), and so was the one with some free time. As I didn't want either of the nurses walking out on me because of her sidelining them, I appointed her Peggy's sole companion for the whole of Wednesday and alternate Friday afternoons – the times, of course, selected by Mona herself. The others – with no doubt the exception of Freddie – were almost as busy as I was myself, and their contributions tended to come at the weekends, when whoever took over insisted I take myself off somewhere for a break. This I was glad to do, as I found myself hating to see my poor depleted Peggy observed by anyone other than myself or an objectively efficient nurse. I did not, though, ever allow a member of the family to take over on a Saturday and a Sunday running: one whole weekend day at least was for my wife and me alone.

We continued to share our big bed, but our cuddles, now, led only to sleep. It did seem, though, as if Peggy took some comfort from our physical closeness. The only time she inaugurated any action beyond carrying food and drink to her mouth was when my arms went round her: usually, after a few long seconds, her arms reciprocated, at first tentatively, then with sudden fierceness. Those were the best moments of my nightmare life, and in the dark, feeling the pressure of her fingers on my back, I could imagine she had returned to me, and fall asleep on that waking dream.

I debated long and hard whether to continue taking her out, and when I tried it, experimentally, and she exclaimed at some flowers seen through the window of the car, her face for a moment showing happy animation, I decided I must take her regularly, whatever my own anguish. One thing she did enjoy – more than she had enjoyed it when she had been aware of other enjoyable things – was her food. So I continued to take her for bar lunches at our favourite hotel, where there was the chance of her face lighting up when she poked inside a sandwich, put her finger in her mouth, and discovered that it tasted of prawn.

Seating her in the window, looking back at her motionless figure as I stood at the bar, how I longed for her to move to another table, and then another! But those days were over. I could, if I worked at it, still extract a smile, and there were still heart-stopping moments when she would say my name and tell me she loved me. Always, for the first few months, Peggy showed me when I approached her after an absence that she knew me, saying my name and some-times holding out her arms to me – some-thing she did to no one else. (I remember my ridiculous, selfish anxiety that I might one day see her holding them out to another person – a member of the Family would have been worse, for me, than one of the nurses – but she never did.)

And then one night, I suppose about six months after I had lost her, I came home late and tired from work, approached her with the anticipation of her pleasure and perhaps the murmur of my name, and met something I had never in our life together met before: Peggy's eyes snapping cold indignation, her mouth hard and hating.

"You can bugger off."

That Peggy should ever look at me – her beloved and loving Eric – with such angry hatred! *This is not Peggy!* I cried inside. It was the moment in which that cry became my mantra.

I was glad it was a nurse in attendance, and not a member of the Family, to hear me sob out that I had never heard my wife swear. I burst into tears, fell on my knees in front of Peggy, tried to take her hands. She pushed mine away with startling strength, and I remember the nurse suggesting I should let her be for a few moments, retiring out of sight. When I returned, the nurse informed me, she would probably be glad to see me.

"You have to keep in mind all the time, Mr Palgrave, that your wife isn't really rejecting you. Any more, I'm afraid, than she's really pleased to see you at other times. She's living now inside her head, and whatever's happening outside isn't really reaching her."

Oh, both those nurses were the best that money could buy! I knew, of course, that this one was telling me the truth, even as I protested, feebly, that my wife had enjoyed the flowers and the prawns when I had taken her out.

"Only on a reflex, I'm afraid, Mr Palgrave.

She has always loved flowers and seafood" –
an inquiring glance, to which I remember
nodding dumbly, because for the moment I
was unable to speak – "and so her reflexes
express pleasure. That's a good thing, Mr
Palgrave, don't let me appear to be suggesting otherwise. It can only help to keep
her as cheerful as possible. I just don't want
you to see it as significant. I'm afraid that
once this illness—"

"I know, nurse. But thank you."

And the nurse had been right. When I had
poured myself a stiff whisky and downed
half of it, I went back into the sitting room
and Peggy held out her arms to me and said
my name.

When I left in the mornings, now, she was
still in bed, and usually asleep. I had started
to set my alarm half an hour later, because
of there being no more shared, leisurely
breakfasts, and I quickly got into the way of
silencing it on its second electronic squawk
– not that Peggy, who had always been the
quicker to respond to it, was ever aware of it
again – then sliding carefully out of bed and
taking my clothes into the bathroom to
dress. It was a relief when I returned to the
bedroom to find her as I had left her, curled
up on her side, but there were a few days
when she would be on her back staring in

alarm at the ceiling, or even propped on an elbow looking anxiously round the room.

By this time I would be able to hear one of the nurses – or Mona – moving about downstairs, putting the kettle on for the breakfast I would always insist on having alone (with difficulty, in the case of Mona). So after comforting Peggy, those days when she was awake, I would call over the banisters and whoever was down there would come upstairs. Always, eventually, I seemed able to reassure my darling into lying back on the pillow and closing her eyes, but if she was still distressed when my substitute came up I found it anguishing to have to hand her over. But I had a tight schedule to honour and there was no alternative. At least I had left myself no time to linger over my breakfast and compare it with the breakfasts Peggy and I had enjoyed together; I no longer even sat down, just scoffed a bowl of cereal, a piece of toast and a mug of tea standing at the work surface while I looked through the post I was every morning thankful came early enough to distract me.

When I got home at night Peggy was always dressed and groomed, the way she was at the weekends and during any breaks I could manage, when I carried out these offices for her myself. Mercifully she remained in charge of her bodily functions, although she needed someone in attendance and I knew that in this area, too, she would deteriorate.

Showering her was a bittersweet experience; it made me so aware of the unchanged familiarity of her body, left helpless by her vanished mind. She enjoyed the sensation of the water, though, to the extent of sometimes laughing when she felt it on her shoulders, and although she couldn't share this laughter with me, any more, to hear it was a small comfort.

During the day, when I was at home, she would follow me about house and garden like a small devoted dog, which meant that at least I always knew where she was. Generally she was content just to watch what I was doing, sometimes humming tunelessly, sometimes moving about, looking puzzled, picking things up, staring at them in her hand, then putting them down again – usually with care, but I had moved a few of our more delicate and costly artefacts out of her reach, feeling a painful sense of betrayal as I did so. Sometimes, when I had managed to absorb myself in something other than her, I would feel a gentle pull at my sleeve, or a hand on my cheek, and would look up into anxious, unhappy eyes. They would smile when I responded, she would nestle against me, and I would tell myself that I hadn't really noticed, in that moment when she so gently demanded my attention, the small, deep pinpoint of anger.

So it was for months, for more than a year, and it was one of the nurses who alerted me to the next change.

When she came to join me in the hall one night I saw she had a long red line down her cheek.

"Nurse! Whatever happened to you?"

I knew, of course, before she told me.

"Now, you mustn't get upset, Mr Palgrave, but your wife got a wee bit stroppy this afternoon. It was while I was making the scones, and I was concentrating for a few moments, not looking at her or talking to her. She suddenly shot up to me and put out her hand and before I could ... well, it was my fault, in a way; I'd meant to cut her nails before I started the baking. Now, it may not happen again for some time, Mr Palgrave, but I'm afraid it will happen, it's part of the syndrome. Well, you know that, of course."

"Yes, nurse. I know it."

And yet, as with each earlier development in Peggy's terrible disease, I realised as I accepted the onset of this latest one that another absurd hope had just died.

Fourteen

On the afternoon of the fifth day of her official convalescence, John Bright reluctantly agreed to park behind his hotel and let Phyllida walk across Dawlish Square to the Agency. This time, when she entered the outer office, Steve wasn't there and Jenny was looking anxious. Peter's door was closed, but the sound of male voices came through it and Phyllida knew what to expect before Jenny's muttered warning.

Detective Chief Superintendent Maurice Kendrick was reclining in the only full-sized armchair, tucked into a corner of Peter's office and seldom occupied, and Peter's chair was swivelled to face it. Phyllida just had time to decide they were comfortable together before both sprang to their feet and Peter came round his desk to assist her descent into her customary chair, a gesture he did not ordinarily make.

"You're looking better, Miss Moon," the DCS said judiciously, when the three of them were seated and Peter's chair was re-angled to give him equal access to the other two. "I've had some belated pangs of conscience about putting you to work during your convalescence, so I'm relieved to see it."

"Adrenalin aids recovery, Chief Superintendent. Not that I've been able to generate very much of it so far, I'm afraid." Phyllida realised as she spoke, with a slightly wistful surprise, that if she had been purely convalescent at Stansfield Manor, laid up conscienceless with the books she had long wanted to reread and the delights of the garden at hand, she would have been content there. It was the knowledge that she was on a job which was refusing to yield results that had generated the sense of frustration – and even, absurdly, guilt – which was denying her the slow pleasures of convalescence.

"I didn't exactly expect anything, but the coincidence of your surgery and my being coaxed into an unofficial investigation was too much to ignore. And you're being too modest. From what Dr Piper tells me, you've had some results."

"None that point to any illegal activities at the Manor. I know there's a man called Douglas who's causing the Director some anxiety. And I'm afraid there's a woman who fits the bill made out by your wife's cousin. But Peter will have told you all this. And what young Debbie said to me the day I arrived about the deaths of residents with Alzheimer's: 'They hadn't been like that for very long and they weren't all that far gone.'" No lines she had had to learn for the stage had come more pat.

"I find that interesting, Miss Moon."

"There is a bit more. Ah..."

Both men had sat forward and were leaning intently in her direction, and it was their reflex withdrawal that alerted her to Jenny, entering silently behind her with the best tea-set, as Peter had no doubt bidden her. As he must also have bidden her, Phyllida decided on an inward smile, to ascertain the DCS's requirements in the way of milk and sugar, pour out the three cups and distribute them.

The DCS followed Jenny's departure with an approving look, then leant forward again as the door closed.

"So, Miss Moon? What is this 'bit more'?"

"It's a repetition of the name Douglas. In another part of the garden, as Shakespeare puts it." Phyllida paused, in surprise at the way she had just put it herself. Either she had moved subconsciously into the role of

174

Mrs Moon, or Maurice Kendrick was continuing to promote in her the uncharacteristic insouciance she had found herself displaying in their encounter at the hospital. "There are recesses all the way down," she went on quickly. "This time I was the one walking on the lawn, and I overheard the Director in one of them talking to a woman whom he introduced to me as Dr Shaw, the other doctor who looks after the Manor residents."

"But you heard something worth hearing before they saw you?"

"Maybe. I wasn't making any sound on the grass, and I stood still and heard Dr Hartley say something like, 'So we've got to make Jor – we've got to make Douglas see how essential it is that we ...' and then he stopped, I think because he saw my shadow, so I had to show myself. He looked agitated, like he did when he was walking with Sister Caroline, but he just introduced me to Dr Shaw and we exchanged pleasantries for a few moments before they went back to the house." Phyllida paused. "I don't know if Peter told you that when I heard the name Douglas the first time I got the feeling Dr Hartley was saying it as a correction for another name he'd just used, unfortunately before he came within earshot. I know that sounds fanciful, but after this second bit of eavesdropping I think I may have been right."

"I think you may, Miss Moon." With a brief *frisson* of triumph, Phyllida was aware of respect in the Chief Superintendent's eyes. "You're as sure as you can be that Dr Hartley started to say a name that began 'Jor'?"

"Yes, because when I thought about it afterwards I realised I'd been expecting it to be Jordan. Have you been able to find the name Douglas anywhere connected with the Manor?"

"Not yet." Phyllida saw vexation pass swiftly across the intent face. "But we're still looking, and now we'll start looking for Jordan too." The Chief Superintendent paused before continuing. "As I'm sure you will. Without taking any risks, and without jeopardising your convalescence."

"I wouldn't be having a convalescence if it wasn't for you, Chief Superintendent. Peter tried to persuade me, of course," Phyllida went on hastily, as Peter's face showed signs of a wounded *amour propre*, "but he wasn't able to offer me the professional inducement."

It was only the second time she had seen the DCS smile, and it was as pleasing a sight as it had been the first time. "Which would prove to me you were a professional, Miss Moon, if I hadn't learned that already." Maurice Kendrick permitted himself to look rueful, as he, Peter and Phyllida mentally recalled their previous encounters, and Kendrick's reluctance to accept that Phyllida's presence in a series of investigations that had exploded into police matters was something he was unable to dispense with.

They had certainly moved on, Phyllida conceded, but she was still wary as she ventured the result of her musings on what she had heard in the Manor's enclaves.

"Do you think the name Douglas could be an alias for a doctor who's been struck off under his own name? He could be practising illegally, or he could have been reinstated and taken another name because of adverse publicity. Which I suppose would mean that some or all of the Manor staff were either condoning a crime or helping a colleague to rehabilitate himself?"

"It could also mean that this Douglas has nothing whatsoever to do with the deaths of two EMI residents at the Manor." Again that look of frustration, this time lingering for a moment under the DCS's drawn-down brows. "The last thing a doctor who's been in trouble is likely to do is to start murdering his patients."

"Unless he's – insane." Peter had hesitated before the last word, and Phyllida, meeting his expressionless eyes, suspected him of just managing to abort the word "Shipman".

"When I arrived at the Manor and was first introduced to Dr Hartley I had the impression then that something was worrying him, so I suppose it's also possible his anxiety is just his attitude to life, that he's always braced for the worst."

"It's possible, Miss Moon," Kendrick responded gloomily.

"Shouldn't we be thankful, though, if that's all it is?" Peter suggested. "I mean, with this woman going over the edge and being due to leave in a week's time ... If your cousin's right, Mr Kendrick, then she could be in danger. But we can't expect Phyllida to—"

"Miss Moon has not been asked to do anything, Dr Piper," Kendrick cut in swiftly. "Beyond being alert, using her eyes and her ears – as she already has done so efficiently – and asking innocent questions where appropriate. No heroics." Phyllida saw the sudden alarm in the DCS's deep-set eyes, and suspected this was the first time he had accepted the possibility that she might attempt to exceed her brief. "If there *are* killers, or a killer, at the Manor, they'll be on the lookout for anyone behaving strangely and that could be dangerous."

"I've learned to look after myself, Mr Kendrick. I shan't try to be clever."

"I'm glad to hear it." Kendrick paused again. "And if you're unable to turn your suspicions into facts while you're a resident at the Manor, are you prepared to go back as a careworker? Dr Piper has told me he's agreeable."

"So am I."

"As long as it's part time," Peter said. "And not open-ended."

"Three days a week?"

"For how many weeks? If Phyllida doesn't unearth anything suspicious and there's no fatality?"

"Can we play that by ear, Dr Piper?" Kendrick waited for the old sense of resentment to flood in at hearing himself a suppliant, but it failed to appear.

"All right. For a time." Phyllida was relieved to see both men nod their approval. "But how will she get the job at all, let alone on her own terms?"

The Chief Superintendent nodded again. "A crucial point. We've ascertained that there's a fairly fast turnover among the junior staff, as there tends to be in these places, not to mention frequent phonings-in sick the morning after a binge. I'm hoping the Manor will like the idea of a – a more mature person who – if Miss Moon presents herself as I know she will – is obviously going to be reliable, even if at intervals. The thing is, I think," Kendrick went on, turning to Phyllida, "to ask for an appointment cold, and tell them you're temporarily in this area for personal reasons and you'd like to keep your skills and experience going. We'll supply certificates and references, of course." For the first time the steady eyes slid away from both Phyllida and Peter, and Phyllida put on hold philosophical thoughts about ends and means *vis-à-vis* the upholders of law and order. "And I hope" – Chief Superintendent Kendrick again had Phyllida in his keen gaze – "that Miss Moon will by the time of the interview have familiarised herself with the theory and practice of EMI careworking."

"Of course. I've already started."

"I should have known. Anyway, we'll talk again about this when your convalescence is over."

"It won't be over as far as careworking is concerned," Peter said, "for at least a couple of weeks after Phyllida leaves the Manor as a resident. Careworkers have to lift people up and carry them about, and sometimes they're so helpless they're dead weights."

Peter might be quoting Jenny – Phyllida had no doubt of it – but at least he had taken her reactions seriously. And, however reluctantly, she knew what Jenny had told Peter was true.

"Peter's right, I'm afraid, Mr Kendrick. And if I do get taken on ... I've one worry I think I should mention to you both."

Again the intent leaning forward. But this time Phyllida didn't find it amusing.

"This will be the first time since I started sleuthing in character that I'll have gone in disguise into a situation where I've already been – very recently – in my own persona, and I'm wondering if I can carry it off. The people I'll be working with have been so close to me as me, and as a careworker I shan't be able to disguise myself all that heavily. I'm not thinking about myself now" – until that moment – "I'm worrying about destroying any possibility of saving lives. If I'm recognised, that'll be the end of any chance of further investigation."

"And the end of any further deaths, perhaps?" Peter looked at Kendrick, who nodded thoughtfully.

"Except, possibly, for mine." She had to

say it, to prevent it festering. "But I assume I'll be allowed to carry my very small licensed gun." Reluctantly this time, Kendrick nodded again. "And I have a strong sense of self-preservation. But I just thought you should know that I can't be a hundred per cent certain I shan't be recognised as the ex-resident Mrs Phyllida Moon."

"Tell us now," Peter said firmly, his eyes on her, "if you'd rather not go ahead. It's your life so it has to be your decision."

"Of course." Kendrick's immediate endorsement was a relief to both the other two. "I thought that was understood." But he hadn't thought, Kendrick admitted to himself, that the miraculous Miss Moon might have some self-doubt about a mission. "If you have any serious doubts, you must not go ahead." Getting that last sentence out was like pulling teeth, and Kendrick had some difficulty disguising his anxiety as he awaited her response.

"I've no doubts on my own account," Phyllida said slowly. "Just about whether I can pull it off. I know I haven't been in disguise at the Manor up to now, but I have found myself acting ... well, in a more un-inhibited and extrovert way than I normally do. That makes me think I'd do best for the careworker as a nondescript sort of woman.

The kind you're never sure when you meet her if you've met her before. Entirely unmemorable." Like Miss Bowden, and the innumerable market research types that had given her access all over Seaminster. "Making myself seem older. My first thought had been to be younger, bolder, lots of make-up ... But I think Mrs Moon makes the first option the safer one."

"That sounds sensible." Kendrick was so fascinated by his glimpse of the inner workings of the processes that had bedevilled him since the first time the Peter Piper Agency had been found to be involved in an investigation which had grown into a crime that he had to make an effort to respond appropriately. "And of course it's entirely up to you, Miss Moon, what sort of woman you decide to be."

"You don't want to put yourself too far off the common touch," Peter said. "If you're one of the girls you hear the gossip."

"You can hear it too as a safe piece of wallpaper. I've learned that several times over. And the wallpaper doesn't have to make appropriate contributions."

"Well, I'll leave you both to settle the details of your new persona." But Kendrick remained in his chair, his face reddening slightly. "Before I go, though, perhaps in the absence so far of facts Miss Moon would give us the benefit of her instincts *vis-à-vis* the individual members of the staff of Stansfield Manor. Are you aware of the smell of guilt, or the scent of innocence, on any of them?"

"I'm sure Debbie's innocent, but all the others are so ... well, so inscrutable I feel I can't get past their surfaces." But the phantom pressure on her shoulder was telling Phyllida there might be a chance in one direction. "Which could be a sign of either, couldn't it? Guilt or innocence? I mean, they could be taking a great deal of care, or taking none at all. Sister Caroline's a walking example of self-control, both the Manor's doctors seem comfortably laid back, what little I've seen of them, and Sister Anne ... well, she sends out contradictory signals, and I feel there's tension under *her* surface, but it's better controlled than the Director's – although, as I've said, that could just be his normal reaction to life. I suppose my overall impression is of efficiency. All work and no play. No small talk from anyone more senior than Debbie. So I was surprised last night when Sister Caroline showed interest in a watercolour I was attempting of a still life with a garden background. I worked on it in the lounge rather than in my room for the chance it offered to maybe gain the non-professional interest of a member of the senior staff, but until Sister Caroline responded I hadn't had any real hope. She's going to show me some of *her* paintings, so perhaps I'll get behind one façade, at least." Phyllida felt suddenly out of breath, as if she had been running.

"Thank you, Miss Moon." Kendrick drew his long legs towards him and rose to his feet. To his surprise, when he was on them, he found himself putting a hand on Miss Moon's shoulder as he told her not to get up. "I'm very grateful," he said, knowing as he spoke that he was finally closing the door on any future attempts to keep her at a professional distance, and not minding.

Peter asked him if he had a car coming for him.

"Goodness, no! I'm looking forward to the walk. Nowhere's far from anywhere else in Seaminster and I don't walk enough. Ten minutes or so when I can only be reached by phone sounds quite attractive."

"I'll see you out."

When Peter came back he swivelled his chair to face Phyllida and they looked at each other for a few moments in silence.

"Is this really all right?" he asked eventually.

"Yes."

"You're feeling better? I'd expected this meeting, and our last, to be at your bedside, with flowers."

"I prefer it this way. I do honestly feel better." Phyllida realised as she spoke that she did. "And I promise not to do anything silly."

"You still don't look robust enough to be on a job. Any job."

"Do I ever?" Phyllida grinned as pink flowed into Peter's face and just as quickly ebbed. "And this one doesn't include any physical effort. If I still look like an invalid it's probably the frustration. Of not being able either to get any results, or to simply enjoy a luxurious convalescence," Phyllida added, on a suddenly unavoidable burst of honesty. "But I wouldn't have been at Stansfield Manor," she went on quickly, as Peter, flushing again, opened his mouth to speak, "if I hadn't gone there to work, so I'm not being fair."

"If you hadn't gone to the Manor you'd have gone somewhere else for at least a week, or stayed at home. I'd have insisted."

"I'm better this way." She certainly wouldn't have been strong enough for Edinburgh. "So let's have no more ifs. I'm sleeping half the afternoon as well as the night, and I'm eating big nourishing meals. That's convalescence despite oneself." Phyllida looked across at Peter's wall clock. "I've got half an hour before I meet John Bright in the Golden Lion car park, so start telling me about *your* professional frustrations, and what Steve's up to."

When Phyllida entered the Manor lounge at half past five all was silence and peace. Sister Anne was standing beside the parked medicine trolley dispensing evening drugs, and gave a quick satisfied smile as she registered Phyllida's arrival. Phyllida mimed a lazy look around the room, then made her way towards the solitary figure of Mrs Thornton, seated in the main window corner and apparently gazing down at a view that looked overexposed compared to the bright clarity of yesterday's. Today the brilliant unclouded blue of the sky was obscured by a light covering of cloud through which the sun shone diffused and pale, so that the sharp contrast of black shadow and golden lawn had faded to a fuzzy-edged juxtaposition of grey and green.

"Hello, there!" Mrs Moon said cheerily, when Phyllida had settled herself in the nearby chair. "How are you today, Mrs

Thornton?" There was no response to the greeting, nor to its repetition, and Phyllida leaned forward to look into Mrs Thornton's face.

"Oh, no!"

Mrs Thornton wasn't looking down the garden. Her eyes were closed and her head was drooped on her chest, which heaved with noisy breaths. Phyllida put out a tentative hand to the forehead, found it cold and moist, and sprang to her feet.

"Sister! I don't think Mrs Thornton's very well."

No alarm, nothing in the wide-eyed face, except perhaps a flash of fear so quickly gone that Phyllida, looking constantly for signs of guilt or confusion in every member of staff, knew that she could have imagined it. "I know, Mrs Moon. I'm sorry, I hadn't noticed where you were going or I would have warned you. Dr Shaw thinks she may have had a slight heart attack. We called her earlier when Mrs Thornton had been sick and gone a bad colour, and when she'd looked at her she said she was getting over whatever it was and suggested we left her where she was to come round. She looks better than she did, and the doctor doesn't think there'll be any lasting effects. Mrs Thornton does have heart trouble, you

188

know. Dr Shaw's given her a sedative and she's gone to sleep. We'll let her skip supper, and one of the doctors will be in later to see her to bed. She can have a little something then if she feels like it."

The lady protests too much? But if Sister Anne had said what Phyllida deemed to be too little, she would no doubt still have found herself reading something sinister into it.

"I see. I'm sorry I over-reacted, Sister." Had she? "And I'm sorry I tried to wake her."

"That's all right, Mrs Moon, it was a natural reaction to alert me. Now, your tablets..."

"It's nice to see you," Mrs Anderson ventured, when Phyllida had crossed the room to the other window and sat down beside her.

"And you. What've you been doing today? Did your daughter come?"

"Not today. She's very busy. Have you been out?"

"My cousin took me for a run in the car, which was nice. We sat a while on a seat above the sea." Phyllida found herself with a fictional picture, clear in every detail, of Mrs Moon and Mr Bright side by side on a blue-painted seat in one of the Victorian shelters spaced along Seaminster Parade, and wondered fleetingly if a time would ever come in her strange job when she ceased to be able to separate fact from fiction. "It was lovely. But the garden here takes a lot of beating. Perhaps we could have a walk there together tomorrow."

"Oh, could we?" Mrs Anderson's face shone with pleasure. "I should love that. I saw the weather forecast on my television just now, and it was very good. Are you going to paint tonight?"

"Not in the lounge, Mrs Anderson!" Mrs Moon laughed. "I wouldn't have painted in public last night if I hadn't fallen for the way the fruit on our table arranged itself, and decided I wanted the garden as the background." Phyllida hesitated. "I'm sorry the Howards are so odious. I hope it doesn't bother you?"

"It won't now! Oh, thank you for noticing."

"How could I have missed it? We can catch each other's eye now, like conspirators, and it won't upset either of us."

"I'm so glad you're here." Mrs Anderson put out a tentative hand, which Phyllida grasped as she started to withdraw it. "How long are you staying?"

"Just till the end of the week, I'm afraid. I

can't justify stretching it out any longer. What about you?"

"I'm not sure. I feel fine now, but my daughter thinks ... We'll have to see."

"Well, perhaps we can keep in touch. I'm Phyllida, by the way."

That was one thing about looking like herself on the job, Phyllida realised: she didn't have to disappear from the sight of everyone she encountered. And so far as Mrs Anderson was concerned, she had been the real self she would be if they met again.

"And I'm Phoebe. Oh, I should like that! I find these days—"

"To the table, ladies and gentlemen!"

Whether it was the afterglow of her visit to the Agency, or her new rapport with Mrs Anderson, Phyllida found herself enjoying the slow progress of the meal and being amused rather than irritated by the snobbery of the Howards, particularly when she addressed Mrs Anderson by her first name and Mrs Anderson returned the compliment. She saw the mutually raised eyebrows, and thereafter husband and wife addressed most of their remarks to one another, leaving Phyllida free to talk to her new friend.

"Were any of you there when Mrs Thornton was taken ill?" she inquired of the table

191

when they had reached the coffee.

The Howard eyebrows rose again in dual incomprehension, but Phoebe Anderson said that yes, she had seen Debbie go up to her and then talk immediately on her mobile. "Dr Shaw was there very quickly, and spent quite some time with her. She'd been sitting alone in the window, so nobody had to move away, and I don't think anybody asked any questions. I saw you talking to Sister," she said to Phyllida. "Did she tell you anything?"

"Dr Shaw thought she had had a mild heart attack, but was getting over it. That was why they left her where she was sitting. One of the doctors is coming back later to see how she's doing and help her to bed."

"Oh, dear. But she does have a heart problem, I believe."

When Phyllida and Phoebe Anderson went back into the lounge together, Mrs Thornton's chair was already empty. Debbie came in a few moments later with a couple of residents who needed help, and Phoebe did Phyllida's job for her by asking Debbie if they'd got Mrs Thornton safely to bed.

"I've been in the dining room all during supper, Mrs Anderson, but Sister Anne's just told me Dr Shaw came back while you were eating and between them they got her upstairs. She hadn't wanted anything to eat, but apparently she went straight to sleep and they're hoping she'll be back to herself by the morning."

But in the morning, when Debbie came into Phyllida's room with her breakfast, she was pink-faced and puffy-eyed and told Phyllida that a couple of hours earlier she had discovered Mrs Thornton dead in her bed.

"It was a terrible shock, Mrs Moon, I can tell you, and I feel very upset. I was fond of Mrs Thornton, she was a really nice lady when she was herself. At least she looked peaceful, and Sister Caroline told me she'd died in her sleep. Well, she did have heart trouble, you know, and her mental problems were bound to get worse, so perhaps it was a blessing."

Fifteen

Oh, but we were blessed in the end, Peggy and I!

We'd been out to lunch one beautiful day in March, and she had pointed at some laburnum blossom in the garden of our favourite hotel and laughed like a delighted child. That evening I had watched her grow a little pale and subdued, but it hadn't alarmed me because in addition to the prawn sandwiches she had enjoyed at lunchtime she had eaten her supper with her usual latterday relish, and when I took her up to bed she fell asleep while I was still arranging the bedclothes over her shoulders. I too got into bed soon afterwards and read for a while, aware of the warm breathing stillness of her beside me and painfully imagining, as I did every night, that because she appeared to be what she had once been, she would waken in the morning as herself.

But she wakened in the dead of night, and

wakened me with the sudden harsh struggle of her breathing. For a few moments the desperate rhythm was my own breath in the dream I was dreaming, turning it into a nightmare of struggling in marching order up a steep hillside in the knowledge that oblivion awaited me should I slip back to the foot – a nightmare for once less terrifying than the reality to which it awakened me.

I switched on the bedside light and turned to look at her, just as she was sick. I knew that she was dying, and that I couldn't leave her even for the seconds it would take to find and wet a facecloth, so I did what I could with a handkerchief, propped her up a little, and leaned over her, stroking her wet forehead.

She cried out a few times as I watched her, her arms stiffening and her beautiful hands pushing mine aside so that she could clutch her chest. When her face contorted with the pain it lost its vacancy and bewilderment and became the face of every sentient suffering being, so that my last sight of Peggy alive was of her old self in agony.

I was unaware of time, but when the suffering ceased and I had closed her eyes I looked again at my digital clock, and the numbers had moved from 4:14 to 4:42. Her

195

death throes had begun and ended inside a half-hour.

Oh, but we were finally blessed! And on her last day she had seen something beautiful that had made her laugh.

I went to the window and pulled back the curtains. The world was grey – it had started its transition into daylight – and when I opened the window the air was layered with the sleepy singing of birds and I put my head against the pane and wept my thanks that it was over, and so swiftly.

When I went back to the bed I saw that in death she had been restored, and that I was looking down on the face of my beloved as I had seen it in sleep over the years. I adhere to no orthodox religion, but I fell on my knees by the bed and gave formless thanks to whoever or whatever had allowed her to escape into and through her true self. Then I washed her and laid her out, and sat down in the armchair in the corner of the bedroom, from where I could see her head on the pillow and her calm white profile.

I even slept, eventually. Without dreaming, but without losing the sense that my whole being was a huge, surging thank you for what had been granted us.

I didn't even have to steel myself to contact the family. I rang Robert first, as usual,

196

and it was only as I listened to the ringing tone that it occurred to me that he – and the others – might not view what had happened as the wonderful news it was to me and that I must not, at least initially, let my sense of gratitude – of joy, even – show in my revelation.

"Robert."

"Eric. Something's happened."

I had waited until half past eight, but there must have been something different in the way I said his name. "Yes. Peggy died at a quarter to five this morning." I remember I hastened on. "It was a coronary. She woke me half an hour before the end with heavy breathing. She was sick, and obviously experiencing bad pain in her chest. But for such a blessedly short time. Robert, I—"

"Thank God, Eric. Thank God."

He probably wasn't thinking about me, but he was thinking the right way about his sister, and I decided I would have him with me when I tried to persuade the others – George and Mona and Pamela, if not the twins – that death for once was a blessing.

"Oh, Robert, yes! And d'you know, I took her out yesterday and she laughed because she liked the laburnum. And now ... She's herself again. You'll see. Robert, I'm so grateful."

"So am I."

"Thank you." In that moment I got nearer than at any other time to liking Robert rather than just finding him the least obnoxious member of Peggy's family.

"Shall I tell the others?"

"You're very kind. If you'll speak to Pamela and George I'll ring the twins. Tell them to come, of course, whenever they want. I'll get on with the other arrangements."

"You're sure?"

It was as if after twenty-five years he had suddenly started to appreciate me. Although, having written that, I suppose there had always been moments when Robert and I had briefly understood one another. "Certain. I won't be going into work, of course, and I want things to do."

"Eric..."

"Yes?"

"The family has always used Bentham's."

"Of course." I remember at that moment having a sudden rush of tears, because Peggy and I, the afternoon before, had driven round a flower-filled traffic island and I had spotted the discreet notice announcing its sponsorship by Bentham Brothers, Funeral Directors, and been slightly amused.

"All right, Eric?"

He had heard the sob. "Yes. It's relief, Robert, as well as grief." His reaction to my news had emboldened me.

"I understand. I feel the same. Eric, I have to go now." Because he was crying too, I think.

"Of course. I'll see you later."

I was glad to ring off, because I could hear that day's nurse moving about downstairs. My dressing gown was new and decent (Peggy would have laughed at me for so much as considering my appearance at such a time), and after brushing my hair I went down as I was.

"Mr Palgrave! Whatever is the matter?"

I don't know if it was the dressing gown – she had never seen me in one before – or something in my face, but I remember hers settling into an attitude of grave attention as she awaited my response. "Mrs Palgrave died in the night, nurse. Of a heart attack. It was very quick."

"And a mercy, Mr Palgrave. The poor dear lady!" I was touched to see that her eyes were glistening. "Would you like me to lay her out?"

"I've done it, but thank you. Perhaps you would sit with her while I make arrangements."

Pamela arrived first, scarcely to my surprise, closely followed by George and Mona. Then Robert, and finally the twins. My relief that even Pamela pronounced Peggy's death to be a release made me realise that twenty-five years with them as in-laws had engendered in me a constant feeling of slight guilt. That I had annexed their sister? And was unworthy of her?

I shall never know for sure if they believe that.

Or if I do.

Sixteen

A blessing.

For Mrs Thornton herself. And for the daughter who had loved her and been made wretched by her suffering. By lunchtime the word "perhaps" had disappeared from the vocabulary of those, including Debbie, discussing Mrs Thornton's sudden demise.

"It's a shame they can't let Mrs Thornton's daughter have her holiday out," Debbie told Phyllida, plumping down into a chair beside her when she had distributed the mid-morning coffees. "But I suppose she's got to be told right away; she couldn't not be. Anyway, she was so upset and worried about her mother, she'll see it as a blessing, Mrs Moon." Debbie sniffed, and wiped her still pink-tinged eyes. "It's just ... When people have gone all the way over the edge you usually don't know what they're really like unless you knew them before, but Mrs Thornton was still herself most of the time and it just seemed ... well, too soon."

"I know what you mean, Debbie."

Phyllida knew too now, for certain – because no unsophisticated young woman could be so challengingly disingenuous – that Debbie was speaking out of her fearless innocence. For a moment, in the tranquil sunny room, she had a pang of alarm for her: if the Chief Superintendent's concern was justified, that innocence, unknowingly broadcasting the truth, could be seen by Mrs Thornton's killer as a danger that must be removed...

"What happens to poor Mrs Thornton now?" Mrs Moon casually inquired.

"Oh, she's already been taken to Glover's. That's the undertakers the Manor uses unless a relative asks for another firm. Usually they're glad for us to see to that side of things. And with Mrs Thornton's family being so far away..."

"There'll be no need for an inquest, I hope."

"Oh, no!" Debbie looked shocked, as if Mrs Moon had suggested something indecent. "Dr Clifford and Dr Shaw consulted together about the death certificate, as the Director always insists they do when there's a sudden death, and both agreed that the cause of death was a heart attack. It's always a possibility when you have a weakness there."

An induced weakness? Phyllida suspected Debbie of quoting and, remembering Mrs Thornton in the drawing-room window the night before, she wondered if her condition then had been a prepared halfway house, an ad signalling the normality of what was to come a few hours later. All she could do was to wonder, she mused crossly as the morning crawled on. But what else could she expect? If Mrs Thornton's death had not been from natural causes, whoever had brought it about would hardly be leaving clues.

"It didn't sound like special pleading," Phyllida said on her mobile to Peter when she had gone up to her room after lunch. "And I'm certain now that if there's something going on Debbie knows nothing about it. She seemed surprised – shocked, even – when I asked her if there was to be an inquest. There isn't, and Debbie also told me it's standard practice at the Manor for both outside doctors to examine the body after a sudden death before agreeing one of them can sign the death certificate. So if there *is* murder at the Manor and it doesn't involve the doctors, whoever's responsible must be confident as well as clever. I didn't ring you earlier because I wanted the chance to observe the reactions – or apparent reactions – of other members of staff, and I haven't seen anything I wouldn't have expected to see after a sudden death. Both sisters were grave and unsmiling – just sufficiently more grave and unsmiling than usual – and Dr Hartley came into the dining room at lunchtime and made a solemn little announcement. He didn't seem any different from his usual troubled self, but what can we really expect, Peter? People who've just committed a murder they're confident of getting away with are hardly likely to fall down on acting surprised and upset."

"You're right, as usual. But on the other hand, a guilty party wouldn't have any idea there's a spy in the camp."

"No, but they'll be acting as if they did; they have to be geared for the unexpected."

"Have you managed to find out what happens now to the body?"

"Debbie tells me it's gone to the funeral parlour the Manor uses – Glover's. I looked them up in the phone book, and they're very near here. Have you had any dealings with them?"

"Nope. But we'll keep them in mind." Peter paused, then went on in a rush. "Look, Phyllida, there's hardly likely to be another victim in the next couple of days, and I want you to enjoy your last taste of ease and luxury. Keep your eyes and ears open, of course – well, I don't suppose you could manage not to – but think of yourself first and foremost from now on as what you're supposed to be, someone recovering from an operation. I know the suggestion's come a bit late, like my conscience, but don't expect to achieve anything business-wise for the rest of this incarnation. With luck you'll be back soon enough as one of the workers. Though I absolutely insist you have a couple of days at home before you come into the office, to get back into a routine of looking after yourself. I mean it, Phyllida."

"I can tell. All right."

"And try to enjoy your last easeful hours. I mean that, too."

"I know you do. Thanks." Belated as it was, and probably prompted by Jenny, she was touched by his concern. "And I promise I'll do my best."

She would, too, Phyllida decided as she lay down on the bed. All it would entail would be a determination not to feel frustrated if her sojourn at the Manor yielded nothing beyond its meagre delivery to date, and, if it did, to count that as a bonus. This would mean she could enjoy the garden, and her observation of the staff and her fellow residents, without any further striving to wrest significance from them. To say nothing of one of the classic paperbacks that had sat so far in an undisturbed stack beside her bed.

Her hour of afternoon sleep was dreamless, and she awoke to unfamiliar sensations of hope and strength that reminded her of how she had been accustomed to feel before her operation. With or without the aid of the Manor, she had recovered. She was even able to spring off the bed without regretting it, and the face that confronted her in the bathroom mirror was half smiling.

When she left her room she was carrying *Middlemarch*, and she went straight out into the garden and down to the nearest enclave, glad to be slackening her determined pace for no other reason than to respond to the delights of the accompanying border. As she settled into the first seat and opened her book, she found that her ears, along with the rest of her body, were still geared to the possibility of being a third-time-lucky eavesdropper, but after a few moments she managed to suppress what was near to becoming a reflex, and started to read.

A shadow fell over her book before she

had turned the first page, and she gave a little gasp of surprise as she looked up into the gravely attentive face of Dr Clifford.

"I'm sorry, I startled you. Grass muffles footsteps."

"It's all right. Is there something I can do for you, Dr Clifford?"

Or you for me?

"You can give me a few moments of your company. May I sit down?"

"Of course."

"How are you now, Mrs Moon?" he inquired when he was seated beside her, not touching her at any point although the point he had once touched on her shoulder had begun to throb as the seat shifted slightly under his weight.

"I'm well again." *And yes, I am* Mrs *Moon.*

"Good."

She had continued to look straight ahead of her, but when she felt him turn towards her she had to turn too and look at him, accept the sexual challenge in his eyes and hope it fronted no more than the lazy interest of the casual seducer. In whichever persona, she was at Stansfield Manor to work.

"I feel very sad about Mrs Thornton, though."

The seat shifted again. A gear shift

downwards following her diffusion of the tension between them? Or discomfort at her statement?

"Ah, yes. But her future was anything but bright."

"Oh, I know. I know she'd get worse and it was a blessed relief and all that. But I had a great friend once who developed Alzheimer's and she was still the person I loved."

"Of course. But didn't that make you all the more glad for her when she was released?"

"Yes. I suppose it did." How much dare she say? It was as if she had two hearts, each beating for a different anxiety. Her own, and Mrs Moon's. "There were even moments when I wished human beings could be given the ultimate privilege we give to sick cats and dogs. You have the power of life and death, Dr Clifford; don't you sometimes wish you could help desperately sick people escape their misery?"

She had gone as far as she could.

Too far?

In sudden panic, Phyllida clutched the cold metal arm of the garden seat.

"There have to be times when all doctors do." Neither too quick nor too slow, with no further shift of the seat they were sharing, but still the same slightly amused voice, the same relaxed body. "And if death is imminent and a patient has to wait for it for a moment, or an hour, or a day, even, of intense pain and discomfort, a painkiller might just be given in a larger dosage than laid down in the scrip. It's a grey area, Mrs Moon – better, I think, left undefined."

"Yes. Of course." What her own doctor had once said, if not in the same words. The scent of innocence?

Dr Clifford was getting to his feet. She should be doing the same, knowing she had gone as far as she could.

In one direction.

In the other, Mrs Moon had taken over completely and was detaining Dr Clifford with a smile, a sigh, and a sensuous little flexing of her shoulders as she remarked on the beauty of the evening.

"Yes. It's glorious." He was settling back. Reassured, Phyllida thought wryly, that he had not after all made an embarrassing mistake.

They sat in silence as the tension was re-established. As it grew.

"The now," he said softly at last. "The present. The moment. It's all we can ever be sure of."

"Yes. And when it's gone it becomes the past. Never the future."

The seat shifted. His surprise, Phyllida suspected, that she, the quarry, had articulated the seducer's law.

"And so, Phyllida Moon..."

They turned to one another on an instant, and joined their parted lips.

It was Phyllida who eventually broke away.

"I must go in for supper. Are you coming, or will you stay here?"

"I shall walk back with you up the garden."

He got to his feet and held out his hand. She took it, and they maintained the contact until they reached the mouth of the enclave, where their hands dropped apart by silent consent. Again without a spoken decision, they went back up the garden along the path beside one of the borders, pausing as everyone did to comment on its varied attractions.

"Goodnight, Mrs Moon," he said in the doorway.

"Goodbye, Doctor."

There was no immediate possibility of regret or recrimination: Sister Caroline was standing at the lounge door, looking uncharacteristically undecided until her face cleared to its normal severity as she saw Phyllida.

"Ah, there you are, Mrs Moon! I'd just

started to look for you. There's a little time before we move into gear for supper and I thought you might like to see some of my work."

"That would be lovely, Sister. Would you like me to—"

"Perhaps you would care to come up to my room? I don't live at the Manor, but I often stay overnight and sometimes draw and paint when I have some leisure, so I have some work here that I can show you."

"I shall enjoy that. Shall we—"

"We'll take the lift." Sister Caroline was openly studying Phyllida, and for a ridiculous moment she feared for the privacy of her thoughts. "You look a great deal better than you did when you arrived at Stansfield Manor, Mrs Moon, but climbing and carrying weights are two activities you will do better not to undertake for the next few weeks. Particularly weight-carrying."

"Yes. Thank you for the advice."

Phyllida followed in the wake of the tall straight figure, deciding that Sister Caroline would look just as formidable if she were not wearing her butcher-blue uniform. The lift had an old-fashioned spaciousness, but the single silent presence of the Senior Sister made it feel claustrophobic. When they emerged on to the landing Phyllida found herself slightly out of breath as she followed Sister Caroline past her own door, through a fire door and into a narrow, thinly carpeted corridor which reminded her, with a dual sensation of amusement and nostalgia, of the drop in the quality of her surroundings on the way to her room at the Golden Lion, unless she approached it via the back stairs.

"Not quite what you've been used to these past few days," Sister Caroline said drily, as she flung open a door, "but this is not my home."

The cell-like severity of the small neat room, the lack of ornaments, of a single jar or bottle on the plain dressing table, would have added to the nunlike aura surrounding this formidable woman – and the only ring she wore was a plain gold one on her right hand – if the room had not been dominated by an easel near the viewless window on which stood a canvas that was a riot of bold colour. Phyllida had stared at it for a few seconds before it resolved into the silver head and broad shoulders of the artist, the eyes wide and challenging and the set of what Phyllida realised for the first time, looking from portrait to subject, was a well-shaped mouth indicating unease rather than the confidence it proclaimed in public. In fact – unless her old tendency to look for significance where she wanted to find it had sneaked up to distort her judgement – the image the painting conveyed was of a haunted woman. And Sister Caroline would have been off duty and out of the public gaze when she was painting what she could see only in a looking-glass, which had to mean she had reproduced her real self, so natural to her that she was unaware of what she was giving away.

Haunted by nature, or by events?

"Self portrait," Sister Caroline announced, indicating the dressing table. "In this mirror. Something of an experiment: my usual subject is the natural world or still life."

"It's very good." Phyllida didn't have to be polite; the picture had power and was compelling her to study it. "Very professional."

And surprising in another way: Phyllida realised as she looked at the picture that she had been expecting to be shown something unimaginatively photographic.

"It's your first portrait?"

"Not quite. I've tried my hand at a small niece, and a friend's dog. I'm afraid I don't have them here."

"I hope you have one of your nature studies, and a still life."

"One or two." Sister Caroline picked up a portfolio leaning against the wall and laid it on the narrow white bed to open it. "These are watercolours, my more usual medium, as we discussed the other night."

"Oh, I like them!"

There was a coolly representational still life of fruit and bottles, and an impressionistic study of a walled garden. Not a part of the Manor garden Phyllida recognised, but it would be hard for Sister Caroline, even when off duty, to feel sufficiently anonymous there to absorb herself in painting.

"Is it your garden?"

"It was once. I'm glad you like it." For the first time Phyllida saw Sister Caroline smile. "I'm better than you expected, aren't I?"

"Only because you're so very good. You could have another career."

"I've considered it. But it's served me well enough as a change from the career I chose. Now, I have work to do."

Without another word Sister Caroline swept her drawings back into their folder, clipped it shut, replaced it against the wall, opened the door and led the way through.

But Phyllida paused in the doorway.

"I'm sad about Mrs Thornton," she said, and with a flash of triumph felt her eyes fill with tears. "And for you all: losing a resident must be very distressing. Especially one who isn't expected to die."

This time she clutched the door frame.

"It is, Mrs Moon. But it happens, I'm afraid, even in the best regulated establishments." Irony? Certainly there was no faltering of control, no panic in the dark recesses of the eyes Phyllida was forcing herself to gaze into with sympathy. "We've had to learn to accept it."

"I suppose so."

Sister Caroline set off along the corridor with no further comment, and Phyllida resumed her place behind the marching figure with fists clenched against the frustration of having learned no more than she had from Dr Clifford.

Sister Caroline was again silent in the lift, and although a number of relevant remarks crossed Phyllida's mind which with any other talented artist she would have considered it polite as well as accurate to express, she found herself unable to speak until they were out of the lift and Sister Caroline was starting to turn away.

"Thank you, Sister. I feel privileged to have been shown your work. It was very good of you."

"One artist to another, Mrs Moon. Now, if

you will excuse me."

"Of course."

Phyllida made her way to the lounge, and straight across it to the sherry cupboard. Mrs Anderson had a glass of the sweeter variety in her hand as Phyllida sat down beside her, and greeted her with obvious pleasure.

"Oh, Phyllida, I'm so glad to see you. And I'm actually looking forward to my tea! I do like good food, but before you and I became allies Mr and Mrs Howard always made sure it gave me indigestion."

"Well, it won't tonight. And so far as they're concerned my novelty's worn off, so we'll be able to chat to each other without any interruptions. Only for one more day, though; I'm afraid. I'm going home on Saturday."

Mrs Anderson's bright face lost its glow. "I wish I was. But my daughter ... Never mind. You look ever so much better; Stansfield Manor's done wonders for you."

"I feel better. And I hope you can persuade your daughter that you do, too." But Phyllida had every fear that Phoebe Anderson would still be at the Manor if – when – she managed to return as a care-worker. At least, though, she would still be able to offer her friendship and kindness in her other role.

That evening she remained in the lounge for longer than usual, opening her book when Mrs Anderson had gone up to bed and managing to become absorbed, so that she gave a start of shock when Sister Anne's shadow fell across it and the nurse asked her if she was going to spend the night in the drawing room.

"No ... Goodness, everyone else has gone!"

"You're not usually the last, Mrs Moon."

"I don't usually start reading until I get upstairs. What time is it, Sister?"

"Almost eleven."

Not too late to ring Peter, but she had nothing to tell him.

Inside her room, the moment she had closed her door, she stood with her back to it and awaited her deliberately postponed self-chastisement.

It didn't come. All that came was an intriguing awareness of paradox: in disguise she could never for practical reasons come close to either her subject or a bystander. Undisguised she could, and she had done, in full awareness that this time, for the first time, she would be unable to disappear.

And despite her extraordinary departure from herself she was discovering, to her relief, that she was still first and foremost a detective. Phyllida got into bed thinking less about Dr Clifford's embrace than about the category he belonged to: was he subject or bystander?

After tossing and turning into the small hours and still with no answer to her question, she accepted there could be another reason for her inability to sleep. It might make sense to believe that Dr Clifford, like all apparently relaxed amoralists, would have a strong sense of self-preservation and would never put his professional self in jeopardy, but at a quarter to two Phyllida got out of bed and for the first time at Stansfield Manor locked her door.

This time when John Bright collected her, he dropped her at home. She felt even stronger than she had felt the day before and it was wonderful to be back, moving among her own belongings as she opened windows on to a bright windy day. When she had unpacked and taken a dead-heading tour of the garden she drove to Sainsbury's to stock up on food and cash. It was late afternoon by the time she was back, and she sat at the kitchen table drinking tea while she opened the small accumulation of post and rang the Agency to report her safe return.

"I feel so well, Peter. Must I really wait a couple of weeks?"

"At least. Which you know perfectly well. I've got what looks like a straightforward case for you that should help pass the time. What are you going to do for the rest of today?"

"Nothing. After I've walked down to the Parade and resumed my relationship with the sea."

Ten minutes later she was leaning on the rail, gratefully aware of her beloved surroundings and scarcely aware at all of any thoughts. The horizon was a rare sharp line separating the blue of the sky from the blue-green of a sea streaked with kinetic white, and a wisp of cirrus was travelling slowly towards the sinking sun.

"We're still in the present, aren't we?"

"It seems so."

She would never know if she had expected him. Seeing his fair hair blowing wildly in the sunny wind, she was aware for the first time of it stirring her own. She had admired his skill at following John Bright's car before remembering that he would merely have looked up her address in the Manor records.

The pang of fear was quickly gone. She had lost her private anonymity but not her professional, and because he would never approach her again he would never learn what she did for a living, and the woman who she hoped would soon be employed at Stansfield Manor was the sort of woman he would never really see.

"You've replenished your larder and probably got some cash out."

"Yes. You saw me coming back."

"And leaving. I knew you wouldn't be long."

"A long time for you to be off duty."

"It's my half-day. How do you feel?"

"Good."

"I thought so. Are you intending to invite me in for a drink? It's a bit late for tea."

"Of course."

If there had been more to it, if they had been in the business of getting to know one another, she would have suggested the walk her legs were longing to take, but she turned back at once towards the slope of her road.

"That's my car."

A long black car parked below her, on the other side. She had seen it without noticing.

"I have the drink, actually," he said, leaving her side to cross to the car. The bottle was wrapped but she knew it was champagne and was amused and pleased. The more archetypal, the less specific, the better.

He unveiled it on the kitchen table, and she gave him a clean cloth to cushion the opening. "Best upstairs, wouldn't you say?" he asked her as she brought glasses.

She led the way without answering, and turned down the bedspread without mental apology, remembering her dead brother. He had romped through the early part of his life, gently and smilingly seducing where he could, and she had loved him as violently as she had disapproved of him. He had died in a car crash before he was old enough for anyone to know whether his life pattern had been set, but now perhaps she would be able to understand him a little, and accept for the first time that they might have something in common.

"I'd deny this, you know," she murmured, as at last they lay facing one another, not touching, smiling.

"Shouldn't I be the one to say that?"

"It would be customary, I suppose."

"Consider it said, then. And thank you. You are without doubt the most unusual woman I have ever met."

"Thank you." She could believe that particular compliment was not part of his routine.

They drank more champagne in contented silence, then dressed and went downstairs.

"I shan't forget you, Phyllida Moon," he said on the doorstep, and she believed that, too, so that the fear came again: because she had made it so easy for him to leave he might, perversely, decide to come back.

"I shan't forget you, Jonathan Clifford." It was the first time she had said his name.

She finished the champagne at her sitting-room window, recognising that a need had been fulfilled that she hadn't known she possessed. One day she might try to under-stand it but for now she would let it be, an interlude rather than a watershed.

And as night came on she realised that she had not betrayed Jack Pusey. What had happened had had nothing to do with him, or with anything else in her life that was important. All it would finally amount to, Phyllida decided as she again climbed the stairs, was her wistfully disappointed dis-covery – tinged, absurdly, with jealousy – that the charismatic Mrs Moon was as remote from her creator as were her old women and her cleaning ladies.

Seventeen

The day of Peggy's funeral was sunny and quite warm, and I remember seeing from the window of the official car taking me, Robert, George and Mona to the crematorium that gardeners were replanting the Bentham-sponsored traffic island my beloved and I had passed on our last outing. Trivia tends to be vivid when one is staggering under a mortal blow – you study the shapes and textures of things that don't matter – and that awful day comes back to me in detailed, insignificant vignettes, brightly lit against a background of nothingness. Mona fussing because she'd brought the wrong gloves (nobody else had brought gloves at all), George getting dog dirt on his shoe in the crematorium gateway and going what I thought might be dangerously red as he rubbed it viciously on a clump of grass, Pamela reading severely from 1 Corinthians 13, one of the least severe passages in the Bible. George clearing his throat five times

(I counted) while offering his final tribute on behalf of the Family. (I had been glad that no one so much as suggested the tribute should come from Peggy's husband rather than her eldest brother: my feelings lay – still lie – so deep I couldn't have attempted to articulate them, and my inevitably poor performance would have been seen for ever as letting the Family down.)

I was glad, too, that the duty vicar didn't attempt to pretend that he'd known Peggy, and that we were in an anonymous crematorium chapel and not the parish church which Mona – the only member of the family with religious pretensions – regularly attended. George and Pamela had turned down her suggestion that her vicar should conduct the service in his church while I was still squaring up to oppose it.

There weren't many people in the narrow pews and, apart from a few of my colleagues, attending out of respect, I hadn't seen any of them for what felt like a very long time. Peggy and I had lived in virtual isolation for the best part of three years, as she became increasingly unable to carry on her old friendships, and I remember the prevailing atmosphere as we stood around in the sunshine afterwards being one of formality scarcely breached by conventional expressions of sorrow. This, at least, made it easier for me not to break down.

I had, of course, said I would be happy to invite everyone in the chapel back to my house for food and drink – I had even selected a caterer – but the family consensus had been that it would be easier for me if the wake was hosted by George and Mona, and I hadn't felt strong enough – or strongly enough (because what did it matter?) – to disagree.

So in the event we stood around Mona's chintzy sitting room or wandered out through the patio doors into George's tidy garden. I remember I went out there at one point alone, in a search for some natural consolation, and found the garden so relentlessly barbered, without a single hidden place, that I walked round it without a pause and came back indoors.

There was no one from my family present, because the only person left was my elder sister, dead since, and even then too much of an invalid to travel. I was glad – in so far as I could still be glad – to have a couple of my senior colleagues there, and they were the only people with whom I exchanged more than superficialities. And, I think, the only people who saw me as the chief mourner: the Family have always been able to persuade other people to see them as they see themselves.

Except for me, of course, but it has never mattered enough for me to try to make them aware of it.

I remember Mona had some rather sentimental music playing in the background – softly, at least – which I was tempted to switch off until I thought of the long and tedious display of hurt that would ensue, bolstered by sibling support. But the most irritating sound effect at my darling's formal send-off was Freddie's tuneless humming. On and on and on. Muted, like Mona's music, but audible when one was near him. In my tormented boredom I went close to him several times just to discover if he really was doing it non-stop, and decided that the only time he desisted was when he was putting food or drink down his throat. What an idiot! As the only member of Peggy's family – apart from Peggy – to lack the ruthless egotism of his siblings I might have liked him best. But he also lacked their common sense and intelligence, and was in fact the most irritating of them all, as well as the least reliable.

But as I wrote earlier, one mustn't speak ill of the dead.

When everyone outside the family had left – how I hated having to hang on to the end! – and Mona, her too young and too fussy funeral outfit swathed in a plastic apron, had begun briskly to tidy up, George invited me to stay the night if I wanted. I supposed that was kind, so I declined as graciously as I could, and Robert ordered a taxi for the two of us.

Amazingly, I was glad of his presence, and asked him in for a drink if he still had room for any – Mona and George had at least been generous with the catering. He accepted a small Scotch, I think for my sake, and we sat in silence looking out down the garden while he drank it and I drank mine, Robert in Peggy's chair.

"Will you ever marry, d'you think, Robert?" I remember asking him. For some time after Peggy's death it seemed to me that anything I said which was more than just an answer to a question was the product of my simply opening my mouth and waiting to hear what came out of it.

He laughed. "I can't see it, Eric. I love women; they're the miracles of creation, which is maybe why I don't seem able to choose just one."

"It would be a pity if your principles made you miss out on someone like Peggy."

"It would, if I'd met such a woman. I don't think I have. You were very blessed, Eric."

"I know."

That was when I started crying. Robert sat silent beside me, a not uncomforting presence, until the storm passed, then got up, squeezed my shoulder, and still without a word let himself out.

And so began, I think at that moment, the cold rest of my life.

I suspect I may not allow it to persist for very much longer.

Eighteen

"Your record and references are impressive, Miss Henderson."

"Thank you, Sister."

No information about Phyllida's new temporary identity had been forthcoming from the Chief Superintendent, but his eyes had lost their straight gaze as he handed the paperwork over Peter's desk and assured them both that all the references could be safely taken up. Studying the slightly dog-eared documents after the DCS's departure, Phyllida and Peter had decided she would be borrowing a real identity, and hoped the lady had retired rather than been cut off in mid-career.

"Maybe the maiden sister of one of his colleagues," Peter had suggested, "who stopped work three years ago" – the latest date – "when she belatedly got married. She doesn't have to have been as unsexy as you're going to make yourself."

"No. But she could have gone abroad.

Whatever she's done, I can't think she's still working somewhere in Britain; Kendrick wouldn't have risked it."

Phyllida had been as impressed as Sister Caroline with Miss Henderson's record, to the extent of experiencing, for the first time in her thespian life, a disagreeable sense of professional fear that she would be unable to live up to it. But at least it had secured her an interview, although merely sitting as suppliant in front of the Senior Sister and the edgy Director was the ordeal she had dreaded from the moment she had first faced them as a paying guest at their establishment.

"So how long do you expect to be in Seaminster, Miss Henderson?" It was the first full-length question the Director had managed to insert into an interview which had hitherto been conducted by his colleague.

"I'm not precisely sure at this moment, Dr Hartley, but I don't think it will be for more than two or three months."

"You're staying with your aunt, you said?"

"Yes." This had, of course, been a problem, as for the first time in Phyllida's career with the Agency the Golden Lion was not a possible official address – although she would of course still be using the hotel to

230

turn herself from Phyllida Moon to Miss Henderson and back again. The Chief Superintendent had been initially reluctant to provide a place where if anyone from the Manor telephoned or visited it would appear that Miss Henderson was indeed in residence. In the end, however, he had been unable to side-step the necessity for a background that was both safe and fitting with Miss Henderson's reason for her stay in Seaminster – the illness of an old aunt for whom a permanent companion was being sought – and had eventually supplied one, an unoccupied Seaminster police flat whose front door could be opened by Phyllida if she was unable to deflect a visit from a member of the Manor staff. She was to withhold the telephone number on the grounds that the bell would disturb her aunt, and give the Manor the number of her mobile.

"And although you are in Seaminster to look after her, you're confident of being able to leave her for the hours you would be working here?" Sister Caroline resumed.

"Yes. As long as I'm there overnight and for part of the day, and leave food ready, she can manage. She's not bedridden and can get into the kitchen to put the kettle on, and the bathroom. If the situation changes I'll of course tell you, I won't try and do what I can't manage. At the moment I think three half-days would be realistic."

The Senior Sister nodded in severe approval. "Very sensible. And we would be glad of three half-days we can rely on. These young girls stay out half the night and then either can't get up in the morning or shuffle into work like zombies. Doctor?"

"Why did you choose Stansfield Manor?" the Director asked.

It was probably no more than an attempt to redress the balance between himself and the woman who was ostensibly his subordinate, but it was the nearest either of them had come to the real reason for Miss Henderson's appearance and Phyllida had to suppress a start of alarm.

"Because I wanted the best," she managed. "And it didn't take much inquiry round and about to find that the best in this area is the Manor. If you decide not to employ me, I shall try the next best."

"We are prepared to employ you, Miss Henderson." It was the Director speaking, but even Sister Caroline would have to recognise the necessity of letting the nominal head voice what Phyllida could read was their dual decision. "When would you be in a position to start?"

"As soon as you wish, Doctor. Tomorrow?"

"Wednesday," interpreted the Senior Sister. "Which suggests Monday, Wednesday and Friday. Would that be convenient for you, Miss Henderson?"

"It would. Thank you – and thank *you*, Doctor. I look forward to working at Stansfield Manor."

"One small point, Miss Henderson." For the first time the Senior Sister appeared slightly diffident. "The majority of our careworkers, as I have implied, are ... well, somewhat young, and are addressed by their first names. In your case ... If you would prefer to be addressed as Miss Henderson, I think ... well, I think everyone would accept that as appropriate."

"Thank you, Sister, I would prefer that." *Because you're so staid and middle-aged.* Phyllida completed Sister Caroline's unintended compliment in her head, relieved to learn that so far she had projected herself to her blueprint. And when she had walked in there had been no look of puzzlement, let alone recognition, in either of the two faces behind the desk.

The supreme test came when she was on her feet and about to leave the Director's office, the DCS's documents safely back in her bag. A tap on the door was followed by the entry of Dr Clifford.

"Ah, Doctor!" Sister Caroline rose. "Allow us to introduce Miss Jennifer Henderson, a highly qualified careworker who will be with us on a three-day-a-week temporary basis for an unspecified time. Miss Henderson, this is Dr Clifford, one of the two doctors who look after our residents."

"Miss Henderson."

"Dr Clifford." Looking him inescapably in the eye through Miss Henderson's slightly tinted spectacle lenses, Phyllida thought resolutely of the image she had projected into her dressing table mirror at the Golden Lion the last thing before leaving: the grey-streaked wig with its tight French pleat, the putty-coloured ageing complexion, the thin severe lips and slightly drooping figure. She was unable to sort out her reactions – beyond the professional reaction of relief – at the indifference of Dr Clifford's brief glance before he turned to the other two people in the room.

"Thank you, then, Miss Henderson," the Director said, slightly raising his voice. "We look forward to seeing you tomorrow." He touched a button on the small device on his desk, and there was a fidgety silence in the room while they awaited the response. "Ah, er – Susie. Would you come to my office, please. Right away. Susie will see you out," he said to Phyllida.

"And when you arrive tomorrow, please ask for Debbie."

Last word from the Senior Sister.

Debbie took Miss Henderson immediately on her arrival through the door marked "Staff Only", into the room Phyllida had seen her and the other young careworkers enter whenever they found the chance. She had wondered idly about its size and degree of comfort, and was surprised to find it to be a great deal larger and more airy than the stuffy cubby-hole of her imagination. It even had a window – too high, Debbie told her with a grin, for any senior staff on the outside to be able to make out what was happening behind it – on to a side of the garden, and a row of lockers along one wall which still left plenty of space for the big sofa and sagging wing chairs which Phyllida decided had been demoted from the drawing room. There was a sink in a corner, at right angles to a small fridge topped by jars of coffee, tea, sugar and a tangle of plain biscuits. One of the most junior of the careworkers was sprawled in an armchair reading a magazine.

"All mod cons, you see," Debbie said, with another grin, which faded as she turned to Miss Henderson, placing her mentally, Phyllida saw with amusement, *vis-à-vis* the amenities and being slightly apprehensive that the two might not be entirely compatible.

"Very good!" Miss Henderson responded briskly. "Do you have a kitty for the drinks?"

"Oh, no, the Manor provide them. Biscuits, too. Nothing fancy, but free. They're good employers."

"That was the impression I received, er ... Debbie, isn't it, or should I say Miss—"

"Debbie! And this is Pauline. Pauline, this is Miss Henderson. She'll be working with us part time for the next few weeks."

Yet another example of the Manor's efficiency: Debbie had been briefed overnight on the new over-age careworker and how to handle her, although Phyllida was inclined to put Debbie's slightly respectful manner down to the girl's own innate sense of fitness.

Pauline's head had remained bent over her magazine while Debbie was speaking, and looked up only on the words "Miss Henderson", her smiling appreciation of Debbie's little joke fading to comprehension of a straight definition as she took in the appearance of the new recruit.

"Miss Henderson ... Well, hello! I hope you'll be OK here."

"I'm sure I shall."

"Coffee?" Pauline suggested, throwing the magazine on to the floor beside her chair and yawning and stretching.

"Thank you, but I think I should start to earn it first." Phyllida turned to Debbie. "I'm only here for six hours and I feel I should get under way. So perhaps one of you will be good enough to show me round, tell me about the residents and any special needs."

"Sure. I will." It was Debbie who responded, appearing slightly impressed. Pauline got to her feet without visible reaction and trailed over to the kettle. "This is your locker." Debbie led the way across the room. "And here's a few overalls for you to try. They're not as cool as they look and you might like to take your jacket off. Here's the key for your locker; your bag'll be safe in there." Phyllida saw the relief in Debbie's face as she registered that Miss Henderson was wearing a light short-sleeved blouse under her jacket. "If you ever need to take off more than your jacket or cardie, our toilet's through there." Looking in the direction Debbie was indicating, Phyllida noticed for the first time the narrow door at right angles to the door out to the corridor. "There's a couple of cubicles, so if you want you can be private."

"Thank you." Phyllida's gratitude was more fervent than her formal response indicated: another consideration in her choice of Miss Henderson had been her low scoring on the maintenance scale, but it was reassuring to know she would be able to monitor the durability of her complexion without fear of being seen. "This overall feels comfortable and seems to be the right length." The overalls were a soft shade of pink, very slightly waisted, and flattering, Phyllida had noted, to good female figures. Not to Miss Henderson's, whose flat-chested droop was impervious to improvement, and for a moment of vanity Phyllida thought wistfully of her own straight stance and firm bosom, currently flattened under an uncomfortable restraining band.

"Yes. It's just fine," Debbie confirmed, an expressionless look passing between her and Pauline and causing the younger girl to turn her attention hastily to the purring kettle. "So let's go."

"We can take up to twenty residents," she said as she and Miss Henderson set off towards the lounge, Phyllida reminding her-

238

self just in time that she didn't know the way. "There are nineteen at the moment. I'm afraid two of our ladies have died in the past couple of months – one only a few weeks ago, and her place hasn't been filled yet."

"I'm told you take people suffering from Alzheimer's."

"If they're not too difficult. We do have a couple of residents with it at the moment, but they've both developed the condition since they came. You've had experience with EMI patients, Miss Henderson?"

"Some, yes. It's very sad."

"Too right. Specially for their families. And for us. I try to tell myself it's worse for us than for them because they don't know how they are ... This is the drawing room."

Miss Henderson's survey of the room had a purpose, and Phyllida was sad to see Mrs Anderson sitting alone at the window, staring listlessly down the garden. The two residents with Alzheimer's were both in the room, Mr Golightly lolling over the mobile table that sat permanently in front of him, and Miss Fingal wandering about, stopping now and then to minutely study the arm of a chair, a window cord or, more controversially, some item of another resident's clothing.

"Miss Fingal," Debbie said softly, indicating the moving figure. "The management ask us to keep an eye on her in case she starts upsetting the others. So far she ignores people, except for their clothes sometimes, only bothers with things, but Alzheimer behaviour can change, and the Howards – they're not here at the moment – have already complained. But they'll be leaving soon so let's hope we can let Miss Fingal be for a bit longer. Neither she nor Mr Golightly – over there – are any real trouble at the moment, they just need a bit of special attention." Debbie looked at her watch. "Teatime soon. That's prepared in the kitchen" – Phyllida thought she noted a slight reluctance in the way Debbie pronounced her own surname in its other context, unless once again it was her old bad habit of thinking she saw things she half expected to see – "and we only have to hand it round. Just mugs of tea and plates of biscuits. It comes in at a quarter to three, so perhaps you'll help me dole it out. About half an hour before the evening meal – that's about half past five – we go round and ask the less mobile if they'd like help in getting to the toilet. Mr Golightly and Miss Fingal ... We don't ask them, we just take them." Debbie's eyes flickered the length of Miss

Henderson's body. "Two at a time, so it isn't all that heavy work."

"I'm stronger than I look."

"I wasn't meaning..." Debbie flushed as she lied. "Between tea and the toilets, unless there's a crisis, you can hope to find time to stop and chat with them a bit. That's what I like to do."

"Oh, so do I, Debbie. I think it's very important. So far as the pair with Alzheimer's are concerned ... I had a dear friend who was stricken in her fifties. She's dead now, mercifully, but I got practice then in dealing with it and I do have sympathy."

Remembering Mrs Moon, Phyllida awaited Debbie's response with slight expectancy, and was not disappointed.

"We had a lady staying here a week or so ago who'd had a friend with it who died, and she felt the same way as you. She wasn't ill at all, she was just getting over an operation, and she liked to talk to the lady who died. She talked to me a bit too, Mrs Moon, she was lovely. She didn't talk about herself but she was the sort of person you just know has an exciting life and I was sorry when she left. But all the people who come here are all right," Debbie added hastily, abruptly back in her unofficial role as PR officer to the Manor. She cocked her head. "I can hear the tea trolley, it's started to squeak. Everyone here at the moment can cope with a mug on their own. If you'd just like to make sure they've all got tables close enough to them – Miss Fingal can be persuaded to sit down when she sees the trolley..."

Phyllida had wondered what her reactions would be to her new role, and was pleased and relieved to find herself able to combine a new sense of usefulness with the essential detachment of her real profession. And when the tea things had been cleared away it was no hardship to sit herself down beside Mr Golightly and attempt to intercept his vacant stare.

"Mr Golightly! How are you today?" Phyllida was aware of Debbie watching her intently from her seat beside one of the brighter of the immobile ladies, and had a moment of awe at a profession which could bring about the complete reversal of her position *vis-à-vis* another human being: now it was Debbie in the role of mentor, herself the acolyte attempting to please.

"All right..." Mr Golightly cleared his throat as he sought to focus his tired blue eyes on the face that had just spoken. "But that man on the fourth floor still owes me money."

The Manor had three storeys. "We'll try to sort it out for you later. After supper. Have you any aches and pains?"

"I don't know. I can't..." Mr Golightly gave up the effort of response, his gaze lengthening to his interior distance in the way Phyllida now found so sadly familiar.

"You're not hurting anywhere?" she persisted.

"Not hurting, no. But I'm thinking of throwing myself away."

Phyllida had transferred a small pristine notebook with attached ball-point to one of her overall's capacious pockets, and was unable to resist taking them out to record Mr Golightly's surreal intention.

"Why would you do that, Mr Golightly?"

"It's time. Getting late. I don't..."

Mr Golightly was so small and frail the sudden coughing fit shook him as if he was a rag doll, and when it was over he continued to struggle for breath. Debbie was beside them as Phyllida bent over him, trying to hide her helpless panic.

"I'm sorry, Miss Henderson, I should have warned you." She was already bringing a small device out of the little man's pocket. "Mr Golightly's an asthmatic and coughing usually brings on an attack. We keep his inhaler in this pocket; he never interferes with it. Now, Mr Golightly, a nice deep breath ... and another ... That's better."

To Phyllida's relief, it was. "Is it life-threatening?" she asked Debbie, as the girl took her place and picked up Mr Golightly's wrist to read the pulse.

Debbie shrugged. "He's weak physically too, and nearly ninety. So your guess is as good as mine. He's all right now," she went on after a moment's silent concentration. "But I'll just stay with him a few moments to be on the safe side."

"Yes. I'm sorry I didn't cope."

"How could you have done, unless you've got second sight? Perhaps you'd like to have a word with someone else."

"Of course." Phyllida made herself circle the room with her glance before setting off towards Mrs Anderson, still listless by the garden window.

"How are you, dear?" she said, for the first time taking one of the hands lying in Mrs Anderson's lap, a gesture Phyllida herself had several times wanted to make.

"I'm all right." The sad blue eyes turned to look at her, and she was glad of the tinted glasses. "Just – wanting to go home. But my daughter thinks..."

"What does your daughter think?" She hadn't realised that her new role would make it possible to override diffidence and ask the questions she had wanted to ask as a fellow resident and suppressed for the sake of good social behaviour. Here was another reason why a healthy-minded being like Phoebe Anderson would want to get out of the dependent spotlight.

"She thinks ... I'm not well enough."

"I'm sorry. You must forgive me, I'm new here and I don't know residents' histories. Are you convalescing?"

The excuse for Mrs Anderson's presence at the Manor which Phyllida had not believed.

"I suppose ... in a way ... I had a fall. I didn't do any damage beyond a few bruises, but my daughter was afraid that another time ... I live in a granny flat attached to their house, and I'm here while they make a few things safer. It just seems to be taking a long time."

"But the family come and see you. Keep in touch." Phyllida hadn't seen any member of it.

"Oh, yes. But they're on holiday at the moment." Or just waiting and hoping that Grandma and a nursing home would prove compatible. "I miss my granddaughter the most."

"Well, you and I must have some chats

when I can manage it. I'm only going to be here now and then, but we'll see what we can do."

"Yes. Thank you." None of the enthusiasm in the face of the woman who had asked Mrs Moon to call her Phoebe, and Phyllida realised what small compensation Miss Henderson would be for the loss of the friend who had kept the Howards and all they implied at bay. There was nothing she could do at the moment for Phoebe Anderson. In the future, either, because if she came back to the Manor to visit her as Mrs Moon she would run the unacceptable risk of encountering Dr Clifford.

Miss Henderson rose on her professional smile and went across to Miss Fingal, who was inspecting the back of a sleeping man's chair with one hand while the other held the hem of her floral print dress up against her waist.

"Let's put it down, shall we, dear?" Miss Henderson suggested. "It looks prettier that way."

Miss Fingal made some unintelligible remark, but let Phyllida take the skirt from her hand and smooth it down over her knees. There were coarse grey-white hairs on her chin and upper lip, tea laced with biscuit crumbs had trickled into a stain on one side of her bodice and for the first time Phyllida was aware of the physical repulsion she had been braced for. In that moment, she learned that careworking was a vocation.

The consumption of supper underlined the revelation, at least so far as the tables near the door were concerned, and by seven o'clock Phyllida was more thankful than she could have imagined to be urged by Debbie into the careworkers' sanctum for a cup of tea and a ten-minute sit-down before the day's final task – so far as Miss Henderson was concerned – of seeing to bed those who needed assistance both in making the decision to retire and in getting upstairs.

Debbie had just agreed with Miss Henderson that it was time they were back at work – "I can't stay much over my time, you know, Debbie, with my aunt being on her own in the house" – when Pauline burst in, breathless and tearful.

"Mr Golightly's gone and died," she gulped, collapsing into a chair. "Sister Anne and I put him to bed, and when we'd settled him down she told me to tidy round the room. I wasn't looking at him but I suddenly realised that awful breathing had stopped and so I went over to the bed and I knew right away that he'd gone ... No breathing at all and suddenly pale and – oh God, Debs, he was *smiling* ... They want you, you'd better go to his room. Oh, God, Debs..."

"Make her some tea, will you?" Debbie asked Miss Henderson, and Phyllida put it down as one of the best coincidences of her life that at that moment another distraught youngster rushed in – a red-haired boy – and Debbie transferred her request to him and suggested Miss Henderson might usefully accompany her upstairs.

"This place is jinxed!" Debbie said as they entered the corridor, her PR role abandoned in her shock. "We'd better go via the office."

The office door was open and Drs Hartley and Shaw were standing in the doorway.

"This is a terrible shock," the Director was saying. He looked more agitated than Phyllida had yet seen him, and Dr Shaw was tense and frowning. Behind them, Phyllida could see the Senior Sister leaning against the desk and biting her lower lip.

"Heart failure, pure and simple," pronounced Dr Shaw. "I'm happy to sign the certificate."

"I don't know what Douglas will make of it!" the Director bemoaned.

"His usual competent performance, Dr

Hartley. You mustn't—"

All three of them became aware of the two waiting women.

"You'd better get upstairs, Debbie," Sister Caroline said sharply. She had regained her unsupported height, but Phyllida read controlled panic in her face. "And lay him out. Take Miss Henderson; let us hope this will be her only opportunity to see how we deal with death at the Manor."

Title of a murder mystery? "Who is Douglas, Debbie?" Miss Henderson asked as they left the lift and started along the corridor. Mrs Moon's major frustration could now find release.

"That's Douglas Glover of Glover and Son, the funeral director the Manor uses. He's a personal friend of the Director." Debbie paused outside a door. "You're up to this, Miss Henderson? I'm afraid it's in at the deep end."

"A place I'm not unused to, Debbie," Miss Henderson primly responded.

Nineteen

Freddie's funeral, orchestrated by the Family, followed, of course, the pattern of Peggy's, but for me it was a very different affair. The faces of his siblings wore even more stricken looks than they had assumed for my beloved's last rites – possibly because in Freddie's case they had had no time to prepare their grief – and I of course strove (it appeared successfully) to match them. But this time I was outside what was happening around me, detached from it, because what had Freddie Menzies been to me, or I to Freddie Menzies?

I don't believe Freddie ever made much impact on other people or that they made much impact on him, I don't think he generated or gave much affection, but he was part of the Family, and any event diminishing that edifice was to be deplored by its members.

And his death had been so totally unexpected that everyone was still reeling under the shock of it. None of them had said so, of course, but I am certain they were grateful that it was me who discovered him. I seldom visited Freddie – his home and his possessions were as uninteresting to me as he was – but we'd met the week before at a family lunch (I was still at that stage gathering my courage to start skipping them in the wake of Peggy's death). The conversation had turned to gardens, and following my complaint about autumn leaves on the lawn Freddie had offered to lend me a device he was currently enthusiastic about for picking them up. That autumn my gardener seemed to be spending all the precious time he could spare me clearing the leaves falling from my two handsome beeches and the huge old horse chestnut, so I decided to take Freddie up on his offer and went round in the evening, as invited, a couple of days later.

It was all straightforward, but I had of course, as a matter of routine, to tell the police that Freddie hadn't answered my ring at the front door bell, and that I'd spotted the leaf collector in the open garage and loaded it into my boot before going round to the back of the house and seeing Freddie in his sitting room through the patio door, slumped on the sofa. The door had been unlocked and I had rushed in, but there had been nothing I could do for him.

Throughout his life Freddie had suffered badly from classic migraines, and although it was not, of course, spoken of, we all knew that latterly he had tended to drink too much whisky during his increasingly solitary evenings. The tablets he took to control the migraines were necessarily strong, and it had occurred to me several times before the tragedy that in Freddie's careless hands the combination of the pills and the alcohol was potentially lethal. I'd even played with the idea of asking Robert if he could think of any action we might take to make a tragedy less likely, but was still trying to find a tactful way of broaching the subject at the time of Freddie's death.

To the surprise of all the Family, Freddie didn't in the end die of an intentional or unintentional overdose of migraine pills washed down with scotch. He died of a heart attack.

So there was no inquest and no media publicity, and I was aware of a sense of relief – tempered by the necessity of presenting the correct mourning image – in the demeanour of my in-laws at their brother's funeral. It was an even smaller affair than Peggy's, as Freddie had not possessed my wife's sweetly magnetic temperament or varied circle of friends, and there were few people outside the family who took up the invitation issued by George at the end of his tribute to Freddie – fewer, even, than were present in the crematorium chapel.

I had been mildly curious to see how George would cope with an encomium that had so little material at its disposal, and gave him high marks for valour in the very fact of his deciding to present one. I should, of course, have realised how valuable the eldest brother's pomposity would be to him in such a situation. His tribute unfolded in round Augustan phrases – Pope, or Dryden, without the poetry – which said little about the particular dead man in whose honour it had been composed while offering much in the way of awesome generalities about death and the transience of life. Looking covertly around me as we rose for the final hymn, I could see that the small non-family congregation was deeply impressed, and the Family itself well satisfied.

Freddie's death occurred shortly before the Family was to put into effect the great charitable scheme it had devised as a tribute to their sister, my wife. I had been unable to escape a major role in it, and I remember suspecting, as we stood – so soon again! – in

George and Mona's house to eat and drink our way through Freddie's wake, that there was another reason for the persisting aura of relief. No one had ever put it into words, of course, but I knew they must all have shared my anxiety about Freddie's fulfilment of his role in the imminent enterprise. They had made it as small as possible, but he was family and had had to be assigned some part in it. Now he was no longer there, neither was a potential problem, and family life in the future would be simpler and safer.

Robert got the nearest to voicing my own feelings when we found ourselves standing together by the open patio door, and I can remember watching a few swirling leaves and thinking about how Freddie's casual mention of his leaf-collecting machine had led to my discovery of his body.

"I don't think Freddie was ever too keen on our great enterprise," Robert remarked, when we had stood a few moments in what was almost a companionable silence. "He didn't like any form of change, let alone anything like the one on the way, so perhaps ... perhaps he's relieved, wherever he is, to have escaped it."

"Perhaps," was all I said, with as compassionate a smile as I could manage. "We shall never know."

Twenty

The upheaval of Mr Golightly's death had caused Miss Henderson to over-stay her first stint at Stansfield Manor by half an hour, but it was still just daylight as she reached the car park behind the Golden Lion and parked the car hired for her by Peter Piper from his tame garage proprietor. So there would, as yet, be no lit or unlit windows the far side of Dawlish Square to tell Phyllida if Peter was awaiting her return and the inevitably ensuing crepuscular drink and chat, and she went straight up to her room via the back stairs, making contact with Reception by telephone.

"Any messages for me?"

"Just one, Miss Moon. From a Mr Charles Boyle. Wondering if Mrs Willoughby was back at the hotel."

"I don't believe it." It was several weeks since she had reluctantly agreed to test the stamina of Mr Boyle's attachment to his wife by entering into conversation with him in the bar of another Seaminster hotel via a spilled drink, and she had put away thoughts of his enthusiastic response as finally as she had filed her report after – even more reluctantly – she had given his wife the bad news. Mr Boyle, in fact, had felt so entirely in the past she had ceased to advise Reception on how to respond to a call to Mrs Willoughby. "What did you tell him?"

"That you'd told us it was unlikely you'd be back in the foreseeable future. It was Sharon who took the call, actually."

"And you're all wonderful. If he rings again, Marilyn, perhaps you'll tell him Mrs Willoughby has now let you know that she won't be back at all." Phyllida nestled mentally into the sense of one hundred per cent security that came with the knowledge that her link with a subject who could destroy her cover had itself been destroyed.

A reassurance she could never experience in the case of Mrs Moon.

"Will do. Are you staying the night?"

"I don't think so." Only if she and Peter got too boozy for her to drive, which had happened just once, when they had both felt at odds with life. And even then, Phyllida recollected, to clear her head she had walked home beside the sea.

By the time Miss Henderson had disappeared it was almost dark and Phyllida descended the Golden Lion's elegant front staircase, exchanged expressionless looks with Marilyn and Sharon as she reached its foot, crossed the lobby, and went hopefully out through the swing doors. Events that afternoon at the Manor had been so unexpected, if she couldn't talk them out this side of bedtime she would lose their vividness as well as the likelihood of sleep.

But the two significant second-floor windows were softly glowing, and she stepped out gratefully from under the hotel's classical portico and strolled across the small formal garden that was the centre of Dawlish Square, enjoying the sensation of her own bodily self and the restored rhythm of her movements.

Sometimes the light in Peter's office window was no more than a beacon, and he came yawning and tousled from the rest room, where the squidgy central sofa was long enough for a tall man with his feet up, but tonight he appeared at his office door looking pretty well wide awake.

"Thanks for hanging on; I was so hoping you would. I have momentous events to report."

"So come in, come in. Sit down and tell me."

It was a long time since Peter had bothered to ask Phyllida, at these evening sessions, if she would like a drink, and he started pouring them as she began to speak.

"There was another death tonight, Peter."

"Good God." Glass and bottle hit the desk with a bang. "Artistic overload, surely? From what you've told me, I would have thought they'd have a surer touch."

"I don't doubt they have. I don't think this one was planned. I think it happened naturally."

"Because it was too soon?"

"Partly, but a bit more than that. Thanks. Your health." They smiled at each other over the rims of their glasses, comfortable and at ease. "It was the dramatic contrast between the reactions of the senior staff this time and their reactions when Mrs Thornton died. Then it seemed to me – only because I was looking, I can't think it was generally obvious – that their shock and sorrow was ... well, *prepared*. As if they'd agreed, when – if – the death was planned, how they would appear to react. It was all so very controlled. Even Dr Hartley seemed less agitated than usual when he gave his fluent little speech of explanation and regret. This time he seemed totally thrown, and I could tell that Sister Caroline was knocked sideways too, even though she didn't of course expose her disarray as openly as the doctor exposed his. And when Debbie and I went into Mr Golightly's room we found Sister Anne with eyes like saucers, literally wringing her hands. I'm convinced, Peter, that Mr Golightly's death was natural, and I think its impact on the senior staff was so devastating because apart from the shock of it, it made them afraid it might be one too many for them to maintain their credibility. I can't believe they were planning another death for weeks yet, more likely months."

"You're not stating a hypothesis, are you? You actually believe that the Manor staff have planned the deaths of three of their mentally sick patients."

"Yes," Phyllida responded slowly. "I do. I've thought for some time that it was a possibility, but I've just realised that for the past hour, since I saw the contrast in staff reactions to the two latest deaths, I've been certain of it. But is it too thin to pass on to Kendrick?"

"Not as observed by Miss Moon. And I think we have to give him the chance to assess the significance of it for himself. I'd better invite him round tomorrow."

"There's more. Miss Henderson's discovered the identity of the mysterious Douglas. After we'd learned from the weeping junior who found him that Mr Golightly was dead, Debbie and Miss Henderson went along to the office. The Director was talking to Dr Shaw – she seemed as calm as ever, but I can't think she could be involved – and I heard him say he was wondering what Douglas would make of it, which seemed rather odd. I asked Debbie who Douglas was as we were on the way up to Mr Golightly's room, and she told me it was Douglas Glover, the owner of the undertakers the Manor uses, a personal friend of the Director."

"Well, now. What was Dr Shaw's response to the Director's rather odd remark?"

"Just that she was sure he – Douglas – would turn in his usual competent performance. I made some notes in the car before I forgot the actual words, and I'll have my report ready in the morning."

"If Dr Shaw *is* in on whatever it is," Peter thought aloud as he got to his feet and crossed to one of the windows, "her subtext could have been that even though Mr Golightly had died naturally this wouldn't prevent Mr Glover doing with his body what he had done with the bodies from the planned deaths."

"Not merely burying or cremating them, you mean?"

"I don't know what I mean." Peter turned with an irritable gesture from consoling contemplation of the glittering sea visible beyond the serrated line of the buildings that partly masked it. "But I do know one thing: when we've told Kendrick, he's going to ask us at least one more favour. So I think we'd better have Steve in on his visit." Peter sat down. "For now, I think a refill is in order."

The premises of Douglas Glover & Son, Funeral Directors, consisted of a small, neat, symmetrical building in pink brick reminiscent of a number of modest thirties-built tube stations on the outer reaches of the London Underground. Two tiny patches of grass and a few wallflowers symbolised a front garden to the extent of just managing to turn the concrete strip between gate and entrance into a garden path, and sparrows were chattering in the one small tree as the elderly white-haired woman made her hesitant way to the double doors, her progress assisted by a walking stick. Beyond them was an empty vestibule floored in black and white marble mosaic, another set

261

of doors and, immediately beyond these, making an almost smothering impact after the austerity of the approach, a plethora of lush soft furnishing abruptly ending the irregular tap of the woman's feet. Flock wallpaper, armchairs and sofas with the skirts of their loose covers brushing the thick beige carpet and looped curtains over what looked like three exits from the large lounge hall contributed to a sense of contrived relaxation so dominant the effect was scarcely dented by the curve of mahogany counter across a near corner.

A furniture shop without any labels, Phyllida thought as she saw the counter, but she remained a few moments by the entrance door surveying the details of the space, her face expressing awe despite no apparent watching devices, before approaching the counter.

Behind it was yet another heavy, dark red curtain and its gleaming surface supported no more than a brass bell, from which the woman drew back a couple of times before with sudden courage bringing her palm down on the shiny knob. The result was too muted to frighten her, but she gave a little gasp of alarm as a figure in black appeared instantly in a hitherto invisible gap in the curtain and asked her, softly and soothingly, if it could be of assistance.

"I ... Oh, forgive me, this is the first time I..." the woman responded in a light, breathy voice.

"Of course, madam. I am Douglas Glover. Shall we perhaps sit down?"

The figure lifted a flap in what had appeared to be the seamless top of the counter and was silently beside her, confirming her impression of a tall, middle-aged man whose physical impact was of such pallor Phyllida wondered for an unpleasant moment if he had modelled himself on his clients. His pale skull gleamed through close-cropped hair, his face looked bloodless, and his large hands were like white birds as he waved them in the direction of a sofa.

"Oh ... Thank you..."

"Now, madam," Mr Glover resumed when they were seated, side by side but with a seemly distance between them. "It is more customary, in this day and age, for the bereaved to telephone and request our presence in the home to discuss – ah – arrangements. However, we are always pleased, in whatever way—"

"Forgive me ... You see, I'm not the bereaved. I've come on behalf of my elder sister, whose husband has a very short time left. She's terrified of the mere thought of death, especially of what happens afterwards – oh, dear, I don't mean heaven, and so on, just ... just arrangements about the body ... Oh, *dear* ... So she begged me to come and see you so that I can tell her ... well, what it's like and what you have to say to me about – about what does happen."

"I understand. The unknown can be very frightening."

"Yes! We've both been told by several people that your firm ... sorry, your company ... I mean..."

"That's all right, madam, firm is all right." Mr Glover smiled for the first time, gravely.

"Thank you. You see, up to now we've been so fortunate. Our father buried our mother and we've never had to ... to do anything like this for ourselves. I didn't marry and my sister has no children so now we have to ... Several people told us we should come to you, you have a very good reputation, Mr ... you said ... ?"

"Glover. Mr Douglas Glover. We believe in personal service."

"My sister will be reassured. She will want cremation, and we have no church connection, so I suppose a crematorium chapel ... I think she's frightened of that, too. Impersonal. The coffin sliding away ... We've seen it at other funerals ... Oh, dear..." The woman fumbled for a handkerchief, wiped her wet eyes. "I'm so sorry, Mr Glover, but I'm fond of my brother-in-law and sad for my sister."

"Of course, madam, and you can reassure her that these days crematoria chapels are far friendlier and more personal places than they used to be. And that the coffin no longer slides away, curtains merely obscure it and it remains in place so long as the mourners are in the chapel."

"That *is* reassuring, thank you." The woman managed a tremulous smile. "But there is another thing which I hope you can understand ... You'll bring the – the body to your Chapel of Rest, I assume?"

"That is the custom, madam."

"I wonder ... My sister asked me to ask you if I could possibly see it? The Chapel, I mean. So that I can tell her what to expect when she comes, as she'll want to. Am I asking too much, Mr Glover?"

"Certainly not, Miss ... May I know your name?"

"I'm Miss Bell. Miss Emily Bell. But my sister – forgive me, again – has asked me not to give you her name at the moment, while her husband is still alive. She has a superstitious feeling about it. I have already decided to tell her that this will be the right place for Henry to come, but I feel I must respect her wishes to remain anonymous until he leaves us ... It won't be long, Mr Glover."

"Your sister's wishes are entirely understandable, Miss Bell. So now, if you would like to accompany me, I will show you our Chapel of Rest. Chapels, I should more accurately say, because we prefer if possible that the dead should lie in solitary state even when we are not expecting a visit from their families. That is not always possible, of course, particularly during influenza epidemics, but we do our best. This way, please."

Mr Glover led the way to one of the curtains at the far end of the room and opened the door behind it on to a square lobby furnished with a wooden table on which stood a plain cross between two brass candlesticks containing white candles that had never been lit. Vaguely classical white busts in the two corners flanking the table could, Phyllida supposed, be intended as concessions to atheists and agnostics. She was briefly seized by a frightening desire to laugh.

There were two uncurtained doors to each side of the lobby and Mr Glover opened one of them, switched on an interior light, and stood aside for Miss Bell to precede him. The room was small, with a window Phyllida reckoned to be on the left side of the building, but a blind was drawn over it and she couldn't be sure. All the room contained was a couch with two more unused white candles on small chests to each side of its head, a couple of wooden chairs in vaguely Chippendale mode, and a 'small unlit electric fire by the wall opposite the window.

"All, I think, that is needed," Mr Glover whispered reverentially as they stepped back into the lobby. "The fire is lit only on chilly days during loved ones' visits. The other chapels are the same. As you can see..." He opened the adjoining door on to the same set-up and again stood aside for Miss Bell to enter. This time she crossed to the window, then turned to him. "Do you always keep the room artificially lit, Mr Glover? My sister and her husband so love the outdoors ... daylight ... she might well ask for the blind to be' raised, and if I could tell her there was a cheerful outlook? Forgive me..."

"Of course." Mr Glover was already at her side manipulating the blind strings. "Your sister is not our only client to request the light of day. And as you can see, we are fortunate in our rear outlook."

The blind slid smoothly up as he spoke, and Phyllida's heart sank as she saw that the window was barred. It took a few moments for her to be aware of the small back garden, formally laid out with four sections of lawn separated by four narrow paths leading to a central sundial. Three white wrought-iron seats were at the outer ends of the paths, set against low walls of the same brick as the building. The walls were partly obscured by climbing plants and there were shrubs in the beds beneath them. The effect was tranquil and pretty, and Phyllida gave an involuntary start of pleasure.

"Oh, how lovely! My sister will be so happy when I tell her. I might even be able to persuade her to come and see this for herself before poor Henry—"

"We call it our Garden of Rest." She could hear the capital letters. "It is open to the bereaved for contemplation and – er – recovery if necessary, after they have said their final goodbyes to their loved ones. The access is from the Main Hall. Now, Miss Bell, the other rooms in the Chapel of Rest are currently occupied, but I assure you that whichever one your brother-in-law comes to rest in, it is much the same as the ones I have shown you. We would do our very best to give him one of the two rooms at the back, but the views from the side windows are not unattractive. If you would care to come back into the first one..."

"Thank you."

This window, also barred, revealed a path immediately beneath it and a narrow strip of flowerbed under a continuation of the brick wall. Beyond the wall, a field held a grazing horse, and the ugly chunk of a sixties tower block was far enough away not to be intrusive.

"We bought the field when we moved to these premises," Mr Glover murmured as he brought the blind down. "As what one might call a buffer zone. We let it for grazing."

"How wise ... Mr Glover, I'm going straight back to my sister now to reassure her. I can't thank you enough for being so patient and helpful, and I do assure you that you will hear from my sister as soon as ... that is, when ... Oh, dear..."

"Let it come, Miss Bell. Perhaps you would like to sit a while..."

"In the garden?"

"By all means. Let me show you the way ... Just come back into the Main Hall when you're ready," Mr Glover told her, when they were standing in yet another doorway. "Ring for me and I will let you out. I will leave you now for a few minutes' rest and contemplation." He bowed and retreated, and Phyllida found herself alone as she stepped into the small quiet place. A dove was cooing, there was an intermittent tinkle from a robin, one of the seats was in bright sunshine and two in dappled shade, and it was suddenly hard to maintain her sense of purpose, and continue to believe she had found the place of explanation for the deaths at Stansfield Manor.

The old woman made her way haltingly to the sundial, studied the unremarkable gnomon, then took one of the paths towards the borders and walked a couple of sides of the small square, admiring the shrubs and plants in the beds and up the walls. Then she sat for a few moments on one of the shaded seats, gazing about her with a pleased smile, and when she re-entered the building she stood in the doorway for a last look, her hand on the latch.

Mr Glover was in the Main Hall, plumping up the cushions where he and she had been sitting.

"Ah, Miss Bell. Do you like our small garden?"

"It's lovely, Mr Glover. And I think it's been of help to me."

"I'm so glad. My card."

The small black-bordered white square was as suddenly in Mr Glover's large white hand as if it had been a prop for a conjuring trick.

There had appeared to be no hesitation in his willingness to show her around the ground floor, Phyllida reflected as Miss Bell made her slow way to the gate. As she negotiated it and looked back at the building, however, she raised her eyes briefly to the small upper storey over the central part of it, blinds covering its two small sash windows as they covered the two small sash windows at the back.

The setting, perhaps, for Mr Douglas Glover's usual competent performance.

Phyllida and Peter agreed after the Chief Superintendent's visit that he had shown as much relief as excitement, and decided that his wife's cousin's demands for action must be getting him down.

Phyllida's one advantage over him – that while he had seen her only twice during the months they had been forced to work together, she had seen him every time they had met – enabled her to pick up the controlled signs of his excitement: the way he tossed his long body from side to side in the corner armchair, the glitter in his dark eyes, the intent, even respectful way he leaned forward whenever she spoke. The relief showed in words, in the fact that he told them twice how glad he was to be able at last to tell his wife's cousin that her instincts might well be correct.

"I must, of course, put it that way at the moment," he said, when Phyllida had presented her findings and her interpretation of them. "But as a result of Miss Moon's efforts I can inform the three of you now – confidentially" – Steve as well as Peter and Phyllida nodded involuntary obeisance to the brief warning in the Chief Superintendent's face – "that I am personally persuaded there is a case to investigate." Kendrick hesitated, and Phyllida watched Steve's pale face flood pink and the hands in his lap plunge down between his knees as he edged forward on his chair. "Unfortunately, however, I have no evidence." Kendrick spread his large hands in a rueful gesture of helplessness. "And any move the police might make officially at this juncture would alert whoever is involved and ensure that any evidence there may be is removed beyond our grasp. So I have one more favour to ask of you, Dr Piper." It was a relief, really, Kendrick decided as he spoke, that he no longer had to swallow so painfully on

272

direct entreaty. "Would you, or a member of your staff, be prepared to enter the premises of Douglas Glover & Son uninvited? I have to tell you that you would have no official recourse to the police if you were caught *in flagrante delicto* by the owners, but I would hope to be able to—"

"See us right," Steve supplied as the Chief Superintendent hesitated, and as Peter told him to keep quiet he was relieved to see that Kendrick was smiling.

"You could put it that way. And I am aware that you could – embarrass me – if you were to tell an arresting officer that you were acting under my orders, even if – as I anticipate – he failed to believe you."

"Understood," Peter said. "Phyllida? Steve?"

Phyllida said, "Of course," and Steve said, "Sure. And I'd like—" before Peter interrupted him to tell the DCS he had a volunteer for the job whom he could recommend with absolute confidence.

Twenty-One

He thought he had written it all out. As much as he had intended, and needed.

But as he laid down his pen he realised with a pang of frustration and dismay that it was not enough. His mind and his body were still stretched around too much knowledge, too much emotion, for them to bear without breaking.

Not that his body would break, of course, of its own accord, although the blood drummed increasingly in his temples, his heart pumped so loudly he had started to hold his hand against it, his throat was dry and his knees trembled. But that wouldn't kill him, he regretted, and neither, of course, would the breaking of his mind. And that could happen – he could go over the edge, and then he would have given up and there would be no more worry – but he wouldn't be able to make any more decisions about what to say and what to keep secret. And he wouldn't be able to feel relief, to know that he could rest at last.

It seemed such a very long time since he had rested. Probably not since the night before Peggy began to draw them both into the shadows.

Peggy! That didn't get any easier to bear, either, the terrible void where his love had been. Each wakening, each morning, was a wakening to a renewed sense of loss and desolation. At least it made the life he was living without her seem like a story, a bizarre fairy-tale, or he might not have been able to bear that, either, in its surreal strangeness.

Peggy ... He still looked at her photograph every night before he lay down to try and sleep. And he had started looking at the other photograph, the one he shouldn't have, the one which, when it wasn't in his hands, still lay safe in the old file that would never interest anyone but himself. He thought of it as his secret weapon, the one thing he possessed which made him feel he could still ultimately be in charge of his own destiny.

The destiny of the Family, too.

Twenty-Two

Ostensibly casual inquiries at police headquarters produced the information that the cosmetic processes accorded a body by undertakers are normally completed in time to give its family a couple of days in which to view it if desired. During her second stint at Stansfield Manor, Miss Henderson was informed by Sister Anne that Mr Golightly's funeral would take place six days after his demise, and Detective Chief Superintendent Kendrick had therefore decreed the fourth night following the old man's death as the earliest that could be expected to be fruitful. All of them had been slightly heartened by Sister Anne's subsequent comment on the sadness of the old dying without loved ones at hand: it could just mean that somebody might be careless.

So there was no luxury of choice over the best kind of weather for Steve's nocturnal investigation. Buoyed, though, by the prospect of a solo coup, he took the dry, breezy night, with a half-moon appearing and disappearing behind thin cloud, as a good omen. He had reconnoitred the outside of the Glover building during the day, and at one thirty in the morning, dressed all in black with a balaclava in his pocket – Peter had made him promise not to put it on until there was no chance of being seen by a member of the public – he drove his small car back to the area and parked on a stretch of nearby side road he had earmarked because it was bordered by fields, one of which adjoined the Glover property.

He had seen the horse in the afternoon, but as he tested the low double barrier of hedge and fence the sudden looming of its whinnying head and the nudge of its soft mouth gave him such a shock that he swore aloud, then swore again, under his breath, at his unprofessionalism – he had some sugar lumps in another pocket, for God's sake, he'd thought he was ready for it.

Hedge and fence were child's play, but the horse accompanied him as he loped low across the bumpy pasture, butting gently against his side. Steve liked horses, at any other time he would have been chuffed to bits by the attentions of this one, but as things were he wished it miles away. After a few moments he decided that a running horse with an extra black shadow would be more noticeable than one that was strolling, so he forced himself to slow to a walking pace.

The field seemed interminable and climbed steadily uphill, so that when he at last reached the far hedge shielding the boundary wall of the Glover garden he felt horribly vulnerable: he had seen that slope from the road and it offered no shelter. He crouched low as he fed the horse the last of the sugar, wishing he could distract it the way he could have distracted a dog, by throwing one of the broken bits of stick that were strewn around them.

The hedge was hawthorn, prickly enough to scratch him painfully through his minimal clothing as he climbed it, the horse chivvying his bottom, but it was old, thick and strong. He was wearing tough gloves, and it took his weight while he grasped the top of the wall as close as he could gauge to the spot Phyllida had recommended as appearing, from the garden side, to offer a sliver of space free of tough-stalked climbers and dense shrubs.

The wall was scarcely higher than the hedge and he edged on to it on his knees, then leaned sideways on its generous top while he swung his legs forward before dropping feet first into soft soil below. Phyllida had been right – she was really something, that woman, even when she wasn't disguised as the husky American sophisticate who to Steve's chagrin so inappropriately stirred his lust – and he had made the best of her advice: lush creepers and thick low bushes surrounded him closely on both sides of the small space where he had landed. And into which his trainers were gently sinking...

Swearing again, Steve danced on tiptoe towards the path, pausing just before he reached it with a dense evergreen between him and the building, which he surveyed crouching by the bush while he put on his balaclava.

Two ground-floor sash windows, both barred. One door. Central, recessed.

His only chance of entry.

He was good at doors, he reminded himself as the moon obligingly disappeared behind one of the small trails of cloud drifting about a clear starry sky, and he was able to see for sure that both windows, and the two parallel windows above them, were dark. He took advantage of the sudden darkness to sprint across the garden into the shelter of the recess and regain his invisibility as he stood panting against the blackness of the door.

It was heavy, and reluctant to yield, and he knew in a moment that he wouldn't be able to defeat it without crippling it. He'd told the Chief Superintendent, of course, about his special skills with doors, but Peter had qualified him by asking Mr Kendrick what Steve should do if he couldn't crack this one without leaving his mark. Kendrick had paused to think, and had then remarked, as if offering a general comment on an aspect of contemporary life, that every public building, as well as every private home, was in this day and age a potential target for vandals or would-be thieves, often young men high on drugs. If the Glovers found that someone had broken into their building, or attempted to break in, Kendrick suggested, they would be more likely to see themselves as a random than a specific target.

Steve braced himself by replaying the DCS's words in his remarkable memory as he worked on the door with his series of small tools. It was a tough challenge, and ten minutes had passed by the time he pushed it inwards, maimed beyond the possibility of disguising that it had been forced open. Kendrick had also remarked (looking beyond them out of the window,

Steve recalled, as he spoke) that one of the things that disquieted the police these days was that so often the young thugs who unlawfully entered premises didn't steal anything, they simply lashed out around them, damaging fabric and furniture in savage and sometimes disgusting ways. The Chief Superintendent had then withdrawn his eyes from the marine horizon and fixed them sternly on Steve, who had silently nodded. Not that he had any intention of peeing on the undertakers' furniture or fittings – he was glad, in fact, to find himself sickened by the mere thought of it – but he had a knife with him, and he supposed he would force himself to slash at a curtain or two, and upset the candlesticks Phyllida had told them about, before departing...

Pushing the door to silently behind him, Steve found himself facing those same candlesticks, flanked by the four doors Phyllida had described. The prospect of opening them, and of what he would have to do when he had gone through them, allied with a pervasive floral scent beneath which his nose was aware of another smell that he didn't want to think about, made his heart start pumping up towards his throat, and he had to stifle a retch. *Before I've so much as opened a coffin,* he thought in disgust at

281

himself. *Pull yourself together, Riley!* But he still half hoped he would have the respite of another struggle with a door, and his relief as the first one yielded easily to his twist of the handle was almost swallowed up in apprehension.

It was just as he had imagined it in the dreams he had had each night since he had been given this job. A bare room, a draped coffin flanked by candles. Phyllida had told him the ones she had seen were unlit, but in his dreams they had been burning, the only light in the room, and the door had shut silently behind him as he moved fearfully away from it, trapping him alone with the dead...

But the candles were unlit, and the door remained ajar as Steve looked suspiciously back at it. The beam from his torch was dazzling and narrow, not the best sort of light for what he had to do, but the overhead light fitting looked fearsomely powerful and it was a relief to see a lamp on a small table against the wall opposite the window. It lit to a dim orange glow when he pressed its switch, but the moon was now shining through the thin blind and he had all the light he needed to remove the drape and find the edge of the coffin lid.

Phyllida had described Mr Golightly as

graphically as she was able from her brief acquaintance with him, and the DCS and the Agency staff had agreed that two thin, short elderly male bodies with silky white hair and beaky noses would be an unlikely coincidence. His stomach heaving and his hands trembling, Steve raised the heavy lid and let the far side of the coffin take most of its weight as he made himself look inside the space beneath it. His first impression was of heavy folds of white satin with something dark at their heart, but as his vision steadied and he forced his eyes on to that central darkness it resolved into a young woman with flowing red hair and white hands folded on her breast.

Knowing that she would haunt his future dreams, and attempting to keep her as insubstantial as possible, Steve closed his eyes and carefully lowered the coffin lid by feel, then clicked off the lamp and left the room before pausing to talk to himself again and trying to still his trembling. The door next to the room he had just left revealed an empty plinth, and as he turned to the doors on the other side of the lobby there was a moment when he thought his legs would give way. He'd faced real danger, he'd scaled walls with dogs at his heels, he'd even come off best in a spot of unanticipated unarmed combat, but he'd never had an assignment like this one.

And now, unless the body of Harold Golightly was lying above his head in the throes of some unthinkable dissection process – Steve's brief included the pursuit of it upstairs if he drew blank on the ground floor – the odds against coming to the crunch had decreased almost to vanishing point. Chastising himself under his breath, Steve turned the third handle and went fearfully into the third Chapel of Rest.

Another coffin here – he had known there would be – another lamp to be lit. Breathing like an asthmatic, Steve swept the drape to the floor and lifted the coffin lid.

An even smaller, deeper centre to the white satin. As the mists cleared, Steve saw that he was staring down at the meagre body of an elderly man, the white hair fanned out – by design, it looked like – above a thin pale face already showing the outline of the skull beneath it. The body was too deep in its coffin for him to see the nose in profile, but it looked thin and sharp as well as ivory white.

As he forced himself to continue looking, Steve's chief sensation, overriding the increasing queasiness of his insides, was relief at not having to seek out stairs to the upper storey and discover grotesque experiments in progress – even, if his dreams had been any sort of premonition, an incarcerated mad scientist who worked on corpses by night. He had found his man.

Mr Golightly, Steve decided, looked peaceful, and there was even the suggestion of a smile about his mouth. The undertakers must be very skilful: he had seen his grandmother in her coffin after a heart attack, and her mouth had still been twisted in death by the pain of it.

But what else had they done? Nothing that he could see, and Steve tried to tell himself it would be worse to go back and report to the DCS and Peter that the "competent performance" anticipated by the Director of Stansfield Manor was no more than a cosmetic job than it would be to undertake some further investigation.

After a few moments' internal struggle, he lowered the coffin lid to the dark red carpet, removed his gloves, and gingerly reached out to touch one of the hands lying as piously across the white-robed chest as the hands of the girl in the coffin nearby. Cold, slightly clammy, as he had anticipated. Likewise the feet, just visible below the robe. The head...

It was harder to approach the head, and

for the first time one of the would-be retches broke free and barked through the silence of the little room. Cursing again, Steve swallowed fiercely, and, on the sudden strength and determination generated by his self-disgust, put his hands under the head just above the neck and exerted the pressure necessary to ease it upwards.

The next moment he was as far from the coffin as he could get in that small space, crouched in a corner and moaning and trembling.

He never knew how long he had stayed there, but it felt like aeons had passed by the time he'd regained control of himself and his awareness of his mission, and achieved a slow and shaky return to his feet. He had to take time again before he could get those feet to move back to the coffin and brace themselves apart while he lifted the lid and put it back in place following one quick glance to make sure the body looked the way it had looked when he had first seen it.

Then he had to go back to the first room and remove the lid from the girl. He tipped it over on its side on the floor, but he couldn't get himself to desecrate the coffin itself in any way – all he managed was to knock the lamp off its table and, when he went back into the lobby, place one of the candlesticks on the floor and give it a small shove so that it rolled half under the chest on which it had stood. Nor could he topple a marble bust, but there was a ball-point pen lying beside an open book on the chest in front of the cross, and he used it to draw a moustache on one disdainful white face, and a pair of spectacles on the other. That statement, at least, was unambiguous, and as he looked from one piece of his handiwork to the other, Steve decided with relief that he had clearly identified the intruders as vandals and need do no more damage.

Later he realised he had scarcely been aware of his retreat – it had been as dreamlike as the retreats of his nightmares – except that he must have safely accomplished it because here he was at home, trembling beside his telephone, and seeing for the first time, in retrospect, the final stages of the worst night of his life: the heavy door shut if not secured, the sprint across the garden, from which the light had fled with the thickening of the clouds, the bare access to the wall easily rediscovered. The horse had been in a corner of the field, and he had managed to reach the far fence before it caught up with him, although he had felt its teeth pull at his pocket as he tumbled back on to the road. He remembered, now, that he had heard himself moaning as he fumbled his way into the car and started the engine.

The final stages? Steve looked again at the telephone by his hand as for the second time he lifted the brandy glass to his lips. When the undertakers discovered the break-in they wouldn't call the police. (This time the noise he made was a hiccup.) They'd make their own arrangements to eliminate the risk of the next set of vandals focusing on a coffin.

So the police had to be called by him before they got the chance. Or by Peter. Best to start with Peter.

There was no answer from Peter's mobile, or from his home number. Muttering prayers dimly remembered from a Catholic childhood, Steve dialled the office, and was about to hang up and dial 999 when the ringing tone cut out and a cross and sleepy voice barked a, "Yes?"

"It's me, Guv. Steve." His boss had been "Guv" ever since Steve had caught up with a rerun of *The Sweeney*.

"What's gone wrong? Something's gone wrong for you to pull me out of—"

"Nothing's gone wrong, Guv, it's all gone just as we planned. It's what I found..."

"Yes?"

This time the monosyllable sounded different and he could tell that his boss was suddenly awake and alert. "I found the chap – no doubt about it – and he looked OK, so I thought I ought to – to look a bit further, like just make sure. Guv!" It was a wail. "I went to lift his head and it – it flew up at me, for all the world like a ping-pong ball! Guv! It was empty!"

Detective Chief Superintendent Kendrick had reluctantly given his private, ex-directory telephone number to the Agency, with the stern injunction that it should be used only in an emergency. When Peter had woken him at two thirty a.m., and explained why, the DCS immediately woke Detective Chief Inspector Bob Hughes and told him to get himself and a DC to the premises of Glover and Son, funeral directors, as quickly as possible (which meant within the next half-hour). They were to enter via the back door, which they should find accessible (he did not, of course, offer an explanation for this phenomenon), identify the coffin of a small, elderly man with a lot of white hair, then locate the staircase to the upper floor which they were to ascend in order to investigate the upper storey. It was unlikely, the DCS continued, that there would be anyone alive there, but as always they should be prepared. And when they had completed their investigation they should remain with the coffin, greet the owners and/or their staff on their arrival for work, and bring them in for questioning.

Kendrick's first instinct was to synchronise this action with a visit to Stansfield Manor by another small team headed by himself; but on reflection, and in the absence, as he restlessly roamed the house, of any news from the first team that Steve's break-in was as yet undiscovered, he decided to wait for the start of the working day to take his own team in and to do so quietly and courteously, in the hope that he might gauge a few reactions before any guards went up. Meanwhile, there was no chance of more sleep, and so he also decided to go to police headquarters and use the telephone there to rouse the inspector and sergeant he wanted with him at the Manor.

Once he knew what he was going to do, Kendrick didn't hurry. He made a pot of tea and some toast, which he shared with his daughter Jenny at the kitchen table when she came inquiringly down. At eight years old she was already a wise enough policeman's daughter not to ask him any questions, and he enjoyed her sleepy prattle without really listening to it, letting her sit with him until he took her mother a mug of tea. Then he tucked Jenny back into bed and sat on the edge until she went back to sleep. Nevertheless, it was still dark when he left the house. He was fond of birds, and every year regretted the mid-July cessation of the dawn chorus. Now, on this dewy, autumn-heralding August morning, the moon had disappeared behind all-over cloud, and until his remote control sent the garage door purring upwards the world seemed inimically silent. As he drove along Kendrick thought of Piper's lad – so pertly young – and hoped his grotesque discovery wouldn't leave him with nightmares.

He was glad to reach the comparative bustle of the station, its skeleton staff more alert than it would have been without the last call he had made before leaving home. After parrying several would-be-subtle attempts to discover the purpose of his early morning presence, he went to his office and made the rest of his calls, then rang for coffee, and was drinking it when Inspector Thompson arrived. He, of course, had to be told why he had been summoned and what the approach at the Manor was to be, but Kendrick didn't tell him the how and the why of police knowledge of the brainless corpse.

"A tip-off, Sandy," was all he said, and had a mental picture of a police stereotype laying a finger against his nose. It was all, it had to be all, that even Sandy was to get, and the severity of his reputation – which Kendrick, sometimes with a vague sense of regret, was well aware of – would ensure no serious attempts were made to winkle any more out of him.

He spent the next half-hour bringing Sandy Thompson up to date with the facts, realising with annoyance as he did so that they were still not much more than nuances. He knew his substitution of the starring role played by Miss Moon with happy coincidence assisted by another of his informants sounded weak. His staff would start to think he had unique access to a breed of super-informants, for God's sake. He was paying a high price for getting off the hook Miriam's cousin had impaled him on, and he would never again allow himself to be impaled on another, wielded by her or by anyone else. That didn't mean, though, Kendrick realised, as to his relief his sense of humour kicked in, that he would be above seeking the help of the Peter Piper Agency in the future – even if he didn't find them already investigating a case that had become a police matter, and even though he knew that his private collusion with them was not the behaviour of a policeman, let alone one near the top of his tree.

Funny thing! Kendrick thought, as he felt his face relax and saw its reflection in the easing of strain in the face of the man the other side of his desk. He'd had a blameless career, almost totally by the book, and now, having achieved high office, he was, in strict terms, for the first time in his professional life misbehaving...

He glanced at his wall clock. Still only half past five. He couldn't remember another early morning that had crawled so slowly along.

"I'm going out, Sandy. For an hour or so. I'll be back by half seven latest, and we'll pay our visit to Stansfield Manor at half eight. I'll be glad if you'll hang around in the meantime to take any information. You'll be able to reach me on my mobile. I want to know the least piece of news coming from the undertakers. All right?"

"Absolutely, sir."

It was a moment when Kendrick yearned to say something light, jocular even, to make his inspector feel momentarily close to him as well as appreciated. After all these years he still had difficulty sometimes accepting that it wasn't in him. The oblique approach, at least: he could occasionally manage it directly. "I'll be glad to have you with me this morning, Sandy."

"Thank you, sir."

As he got to his feet Kendrick saw with pleasure that he had found his mark. DI Thompson had flushed and was smiling. Perhaps he wasn't quite the cold fish he suspected his force found him. But of course he would never know.

He drove out of Seaminster west along the coast road, and parked above the first stretch of shore faced by dunes instead of buildings. Then, after making sure that his mobile phone was switched on, he descended some broken stone steps down on to the sand, pushed his shoes and socks into a wide crack at their base, and started walking.

The tide was way out, and when he had ploughed a few paces towards it he found firm sand and began to stride out, parallel to the water's edge, into the crescendoing splendour of a red sunrise, raying out above the distant black outline of Great Hill. He walked for an hour, in a straight line, and on the way back he paddled at the edge of the incoming tide, trying consciously to warm the inner coldness he felt amid the expanding brilliance, and wiping his feet with a handkerchief before putting his shoes and socks back on and getting into his car.

There was no doubt, as he parked it in his reserved place outside the station, that he felt more solid in mind and body than he had felt when he had set out, more ready to tackle his delicate mission to Stansfield Manor nursing home. Having rung through to the DCI at the undertakers and learned that the owners and staff had not yet shown, he summoned DI Thompson and DS Frank Butler, feeling a moment of curiosity as to the terms in which the DI had briefed the DS. At least Frank's earnest young face looked interested rather than puzzled.

It was just short of a quarter to nine when they turned the curve of the drive to the Manor and found a parking place close to the building. DS Butler was driving, and Kendrick saw his face fall as he told him to stay where he was.

"Sorry, Frank." That was Sandy Thompson.

The handsome front door failed to yield to a push, and Sandy obeyed the injunction to ring the brass bell. A young woman in a pink overall appeared, prompt and smiling.

"Can I help you?"

They held out their IDs, gave their names and rank. DI Thompson said they'd be obliged if they could have a word with Dr Hartley.

"I should think so," she said, eyes widening but appearing unfazed as she stepped aside to let them pass into the hall. "Sister Anne's on duty. I'll just get her."

"Nice," Sandy murmured as they looked around. The reception desk was unmanned, but everywhere else looked immaculately ready for the day. They hadn't had time to take in much detail when a middle-aged woman with a collapsed figure emphasised by the belted dark blue uniform she was wearing came bustling up to them. Her eyes, too, were wide and her round pale face, blotched with pink, was nervous and wary.

"Cathy tells me ... Police officers?"

"That's right, Mrs ... ?" DI Thompson paused politely.

"I'm known as Sister Anne. Can I help you?"

"We need to see Dr Hartley," Kendrick told her, grateful, for the umpteenth time in his working life, for the rich, deep timbre of his voice.

"Dr Hartley?" The way she started reminded him of a nervous filly. "I'm afraid he's not well. He left a note outside his room last night to say he didn't want to be disturbed this morning. So I can't—"

"I'm sorry, Sister," DI Thompson cut in. "But it's very important that we see him and I'm afraid he will have to be disturbed. So if you will just show us the way to his room..."

"I can't—"

"You can, and you will, I'm afraid," Kendrick said. "Now, will you lead the way?"

"If I could just find Sister—"

"Afterwards. When you've taken us to Dr Hartley."

Sister Anne turned on a gesture of despair, and Kendrick saw the panic in her eyes. Whatever it was, she was a party to it. "This way, then."

She led them in silence to the lift, which made Kendrick think of the lift at the Peter Piper Agency, and in silence they ascended. A little way along the wide first-floor corridor she stopped and knocked on a door marked "Private". There was no response, nor when she knocked again, harder. She then called out, knocking again, "Dr Hartley! Please, Dr Hartley, I'm sorry, but I have to see you." She paused. "It's the police!"

Still no response from inside the room, and Sister Anne turned to the two policemen, her face a mask of panic. "He must be really ill!"

"You've a master key?" Kendrick suggested.

She looked shocked. "Yes, but we'd never..."

"There's always a first time," the DI said. "Please open the door."

Another woman in a blue uniform, impressively tall and austere-faced, her white hair crowned, like the Queen's, with two small symmetrical curls that made Kendrick think of horns, arrived on the landing as the door opened, and made to enter with the policemen.

"I'm sorry," Kendrick said, glad to be six foot four. "I'm afraid we have to ask you to wait outside." He closed the door on them, side by side and variously expressing outrage, and locked it before turning round.

"Dear God, sir!"

Sandy Thompson had crossed the room to the bed and was gazing down on the man lying so neatly on his back, his hands folded across the open book that lay on the tidy turndown of the top sheet. A pair of spectacles, an empty glass, a nearly empty whisky bottle and an old-fashioned pill bottle could just be made out through the gloom on a bedside table. How many blister packs had he plundered? Kendrick wondered as DI Thompson drew back the curtains and he saw that the bottle was empty, too.

"He's dead," he said, after a quick, non-intrusive investigation. DI Thompson's mobile was already in his hand. "Call the troops in, Sandy, and get DS Butler out of the car and taking up a stand just inside the front door. Lock up after me and wait with Dr Hartley for the team. I trust he won't give you bad dreams."

"Certainly not, sir."

Hoping his DI was as unqueasy as he was making himself sound, Kendrick went out into the corridor and told the two indignant women that Dr Hartley was dead.

There was no doubt, it seemed to him, of their surprise, but he was unable to detect emotion in either. He asked them to take him to the Director's office, where the three of them would await the arrival of the scenes of crime officer, the police doctor and the forensic team, after which questions would begin to be asked and answered.

It was Sandy Thompson, feeling suddenly very squeamish indeed, who found the photograph. He had been forced to sit down suddenly on the nearest chair and put his head between his knees. The floor beside the bed was his immediate field of vision, and it was while he was perforce staring at it that he noticed the white rectangle beneath it, lying face down.

In Peter's office the next morning, Detective Chief Superintendent Kendrick put the photograph into Phyllida's hand and asked her what she made of it.

"It's ... it's ... Goodness, there's Dr Hartley. And that looks like Sister Caroline. And Sister Anne ... I don't recognise the man with all the black hair, but that's Dr Shaw. And there's – Dr Clifford. All younger, that's why I didn't immediately ... I don't recognise the children. Nor the prettiest of the women. Nor the background. And ... I don't know, but it's not just that they're younger, they just aren't a group photograph of the staff at the Manor. It's weird."

"Look at the back."

When she turned the photograph over Phyllida saw the handwritten caption "The Menzies Family, March 1991", and let the photograph fall on to Peter's desk as she stared at Kendrick.

"What does it mean?"

"This will tell you." Kendrick put a hardback notebook on the desk beside the photograph. "Read it for yourself – you've earned the privilege. But let me have it back by tomorrow; I shouldn't be letting it out of my sight. I'll expect you both in my office at ten."

"Your assignment for today," Peter told Phyllida, "is to take the book home with you and read it."

"It won't take long," Kendrick said. "An hour or two and you'll be through. But you'll probably be glad of another hour or two to take it in. I suggest by the sea; it's a nice day."

Twenty-Three

I've decided to tell the story to the end.
The very end.

This does not mean that I am finally betraying the Family (not that I would care, now, if I were), because whoever finds this book – and the photograph – will be a member of it, as only the Family have access to the second key of the door I have just locked.

I am writing because I have to, but I don't dislike the thought of the Family reading it before they destroy it, and learning what their amenable brother-in-law really thinks of them.

Amenable as I was, and have continued to be – in some ways to my regret, but it is my nature – they know as well as I do that the Great Charitable Enterprise (we have always referred to it as our GCE) could never have been embarked on without me. It is simply their inborn sense of their own superiority that has continued to ensure that they treat me as an inferior being.

The idea was theirs, of course. Another family trait is that the vacuum which nature abhors – in this case the death of my wife, their beloved sister – is equally abhorred by the Menzies clan and Must Be Filled.

But it was far more than that, of course. Not a desire for fame or fortune, and in the nature of the enterprise my research will have to be presented anonymously. No, their belief in their strength as a unit needs no outside support: they are impregnable in their oneness, and Peggy was part of it. So her suffering was theirs by association, and shocked them into the outrageous move they made because it was the suffering of them all. There was also, I must say fairly, the instinct which is present also in me and which enabled me to do their bidding: the instinct of all good doctors to seek the means of combating disease. And this particular disease had become, for the Family, an evil adversary on which they felt compelled to seek revenge.

The word "charitable" was employed from the start. And, as George expounded in his usual pompous way, we would in fact be carrying out not one but two acts of charity. We would be painlessly despatching those whose quality of life had already deserted them, and we would be making use of them in death to investigate, with a view to eliminating, the causes of the dreadful disease that had destroyed a member of the Family.

Freda and Robert are doctors; Pamela and Mona staff nurses; I am a surgeon, capable of wielding what George consistently refers to as the Noble Knife. And George himself is a businessman with several successful enterprises under his belt and seemingly inexhaustible resilience.

The whole team, ready and waiting. Members of one family.

I was shocked when the GCE was suggested, and am shocked still. Shocked, at last, into this no longer supportable mental and physical disarray. Not, I think, by any moral scruples, as I have had no part in the deaths and have found myself unable to feel that I am violating my Hippocratic Oath. Maybe by the sheer arrogance of it, the awareness that we are playing God, and the knowledge that we are walking a perpetual tightrope. The natural death of Mr Golightly so soon after the arranged death of Mrs Thornton has dismayed us all, but it has terrified me. Losing my nerve, George and Pamela – and probably Robert – would no doubt call it. Perhaps they are right. I could not endure the hardship, or the ignominy, of being sent to prison.

The terrible coincidence of Mr Golightly's death seems to have been absorbed already by the Family. But someone – I think it was Freda – said at the beginning that in our favour is the fact that relatives are always so relieved, in the midst of their sorrow, when their loved one's suffering comes to an end that the possibility of the death being un-natural doesn't enter their minds – or, if it does, is hastily dismissed. It is a Blessed Release, and as such is to be given an unqualified welcome. And everyone secretly believes that doctors are prepared to be illegally merciful in unspecified areas. May-be that is so, but there is no species of re-assurance that can reach me now.

My skills are not suffering. I continue to do the work I have agreed to do on the poor diminished brains, writing up my notes and giving them to Freda to turn into an elegant Paper. I am confident that I have already added to the sum of current knowledge of this dread disease, but the Family will have no choice, as I have said, but to offer the Paper anonymously and only, I would say, after they have vacated the Manor and this area and returned to their natal selves. However, having achieved the matter I have no interest in the manner, knowing as I do that whatever I think of the Family as individual people they will faithfully carry the banner of my research and findings until it is offered on the universal altar of medical knowledge.

I'm allowing myself, now, with the suddenly calm spirit of a man without a future, to look back with amusement rather than my customary shudder over the whole surreal process ... Those early sessions, when we were selecting our new identities! We each changed our own, subject to the satisfaction of the others. Robert to Dr Jonathan Clifford, Freda to Dr Agnes Shaw. First names were the hardest to decide on and to use, except for Pamela and Mona as Sisters Caroline and Anne. Pamela is loving her new identity; she has come into her own at last. Mona has demons, I see them sometimes in her wide eyes, but I suspect her compensation is that it makes her feel she's back on stage pre-George, if no longer a soubrette. Freda has ditched her husband and is strolling through her new incarnation the way she strolled through the old. Robert is still precisely Robert. I think George is even more pompous then he used to be, perhaps to compensate for the loss of all that protective patriarchal hair. And I suspect that my own forced abandonment of my contact lenses and reluctant reversion to spectacles has added to my anxiety, to say nothing of this ridiculous little Hitler moustache. We agreed there would be no occasion, public or private, when we would refer to one another by our given names, and I think I have been the only one of us to make the odd mistake – not being of the blood, I don't possess the icy command of mind and emotions that characterises the monstrous Menzies Family.

Oh Peggy, my love and my life! Do I include you among your brothers and sisters? No. I recognise that their particular cherishing love for you was because they, too, knew you were the only member of the Family who lacked the Menzies arrogant self-confidence.

The Menzies clannishness was an asset when it came to the move. None of them (including, this time, myself, because it had been Peggy rather than I who had attracted the people I now scarcely ever saw) turned out to have real friends outside the family circle, only acquaintances and colleagues, so we were able to escape the danger of people wanting to keep in touch so keenly they would try to trace us. How we vanished was by telling people we were starting our new lives in rented accommodation, or staying with friends, and that we would let them know our new addresses and circumstances as soon as we were settled. This left the onus of continuity with ourselves, and of course in every case we let it slide.

Robert was consultant physician at the hospital where I was senior surgeon, so we pre-empted any comments on the fact of our leaving our posts at the same time by joking about the extraordinary coincidence of it. To announce that one was going to another job would have entailed unsustainable lies, and so I was taking early retirement and Robert was going abroad for a self-awarded sabbatical. Pamela was retiring, Mona's husband's work was taking them to London, as was Freda's (there was no fear of a cross-check here), and George had decided to sell up and take his leisure near a member of his family (they laughed about this) in the Home Counties. Which was where Mona came from and where Pamela and Freda were at school, so that the senior staff of Stansfield Manor do not have a uniform Edinburgh accent. I, indeed, hail from Yorkshire, and it can still just be heard in my voice.

I think the Family actually contrived to enjoy itself, planning the details of its new life, committing its new selves to memory.

Even I found myself entering almost pleasurably into the charade, although I lack the instinct that sends them seeking – and finding – therapy in action.

I was to be the apparent head of the new set-up – to their credit, I never saw so much as a smile at this most risibly erroneous part of the charade. It was decided, when we found the Manor (we had agreed that in the first instance we would look only along the south coast, and struck lucky within weeks), that it should be purchased in my name, but with a host of checks and balances to offset appearances, all locked away in our bank vaults. I didn't care, one way or the other, because since Peggy's death I have been unable to care about anything.

So to those who seek – and why, in effect, should anyone seek to delve into the origins of such a well-run, well-appointed institution? – they will find that Dr Charles Hartley is the onlie begetter of Stansfield Manor as it is today: a fashionable nursing home in a prosperous area of the south coast of England, well deserving of its popularity. It is, of course, the Family, with their terrifying competence, who have established this reputation and who maintain it. At the Manor the Director is a figurehead, and it is only upstairs at Glover and Son that I come into my own.

I have worked, up till now, on half a dozen brains, sufficient to enable me to present valuable findings. (If I were to say this at a Family conclave, George would immediately intone the second benefit of the GCE: the rescue of our subjects from the fate worse than death and the solace of their families, as if my statement had pressed a corrective button somewhere in his own – limited – cortex.) There is more, of course, much more, that I could do if more material were available, but today I handed Freda sufficient data to enable her to complete the Paper, and I have the sense that my work is done.

I am writing tonight because I have a sudden, terrible sense of urgency. My mother was supposed – by my family – to have second sight, and I have suspected through small instances over the years that I have inherited something of it. And that something is telling me, insistently, that it is time to go.

Oh, yes, there is one more thing I should set down, something that shows conclusively, I must accept, that my qualms now can have little to do with moral scruples.

I killed Freddie.

I was reluctant to embark on the GCE,

310

but having agreed to play the major – the enabling – role in it, I became anxious about Freddie. And I was aware that the other members of the Family, blinkered though they were by their blood ties, shared something of that anxiety. However we tried to fit Freddie into our scheme – or to leave him safely out of it – he would have been our weak link, liable always, especially when in drink, to destroy our enterprise.

Freddie himself gave me the idea and the opportunity, when he offered to lend me his device for picking up autumn leaves. (He was right, it worked well.) In the short interval between his offering of the device and my going to collect it, I worked out the details of his murder, given the circumstances in which I hoped to find him. I chose an evening, of course, and when he came, slow and stumbling, to let me in I knew that those circumstances were right.

There was a half-empty bottle of whisky on the table beside his chair, and I had come armed with a large dose of elixir of digoxin – lethal in large quantities even to those who are prescribed it, and Freddie was not one of them. He showed me the leaf-collecting device, tried and failed to pick it up, and shambled round the side of his house behind me while I carried it to my car and stowed it in the boot. Then we went back into the house and he poured us both a scotch – his, I noticed, considerably larger than mine. I would have managed it anyway, but he made things easier still, when he had put the bottle down, by mumbling that he needed a pee and leaving me on my own for a couple of minutes. Transferring the liquid solution from my bottle to his glass was child's play, and when he returned he immediately drained the glass without noticing the slight yellowed cloudiness of its contents. While he was dying I took his glass into the kitchen, carefully washed it, then brought it back and poured another stiff measure of scotch, which I set beside him before checking he was dead and ringing the police.

I'm vaguely curious as to how the Family will react to this revelation. I suspect I may have won from them in death the respect they have denied me in life, but it doesn't matter to me one way or the other. All my panic and all my pain, I am aware in this moment, come from living without the other half of me, Peggy my beloved.

So I am no longer going to.

Twenty-Four

"So would you say he was mad, sir?"

A call to Detective Chief Superintendent Kendrick by Phyllida – with Peter's blessing – just before they left for police head-quarters had secured Steve a place at the DCS's desk. Not only was she anxious to raise his uncharacteristically stricken spirits, she saw it as mere justice given that he had been the one to stare the ultimate vital evidence in its unseeing face and at so un-nerving an angle.

In true ex-Londoner style, Steve accepted the invitation without letting his elation show, and anyway it remained tempered by the other reason for his sombre and un-accustomed thoughtfulness. The idea of the most disgusting act a vandal might commit inside an invaded premises had given him back a memory he had managed totally to repress: he himself had once peed very much in the wrong place. Sent against his will to have tea *à deux* with a Violet Elizabeth Bott look-alike and behave-alike, he'd urinated on to the smug china face of her most treasured doll. At least the sense of shame he was aware of this morning showed how far he had come since his tearaway days, but it was still uncomfortable.

As was his knowledge, the moment he had spoken, that he was the last person in the DCS's office who should have opened the verbal post-mortem.

He was aware of both Peter and Phyllida shifting sharply to each side of him, but to his relief the DCS himself appeared unfazed and answered him as if one of the other two had asked the question.

"I should say that anyone so violently un-balanced by the death of a loved one must always have been potentially insane." Kendrick tried not to think of the ill-suppressed relief in the faces of his men when the news got about that he and Miriam were back together. "A complex man, certainly, capable of such outrageous deeds and trembling in his shoes as he carried them out."

"His hands didn't tremble, apparently," Phyllida said.

"It seems not. We can already confirm that he held a consultant post and had a good reputation."

"I wonder how his life would have been

outside the clutches of the Family," Phyllida mused aloud. "What will happen to them, Mr Kendrick?" The thought of Dr Clifford – Dr Robert Menzies – behind bars gave her a short, sharp jolt of pain. "I mean, what sort of charges will you bring?"

The DCS smiled one of his rare smiles and pushed a hand through his thick dark hair. "Murder, first and foremost. An exhumation order has already gone out on Mrs Thornton, and our questioning of the Manor staff should give us the information we need to exhume the other bodies – none of them is attempting to deny what was done. Which gives us a bit of time to think about the supplementary charges."

"Violating corpses?" Steve asked with relish, forgetting himself again.

Peter tutted, but the DCS was still smiling. "Not in so many words. But yes, that is a criminal offence."

"Their dedication was awesome," Phyllida said. "And their confidence. Mrs Moon's comments to the Senior Sister and Dr Clifford – Dr Robert Menzies – went to the bone, but they just bounced off. The only thing that got to them was Mr Golightly's unplanned death. Reading Dr Palgrave's diary, whatever he said about being unable to live without his wife, I think he broke because he lacked their sense of mission and was just swept along by the family tide."

"Until he drowned," Steve completed.

"Yes." Phyllida was thinking aloud. "It's a paradox, isn't it? He was the underdog, but he was the one they couldn't have done it without, and he was the one who eventually betrayed them."

"No," Kendrick heard himself responding. "That was you. If you hadn't got me there precisely when you did, the Family would have used the second key to the Director's room and no one outside the Manor would ever have seen either the diary or the photograph."

There was a short silence before Phyllida spoke again.

"George," she said. "I've got a visual memory, and when I heard the beginning of the name as 'Jor' that was it, I couldn't think of it any other way. And I suppose I prevented any of you seeing it as it was, because of spelling you out those three letters."

"You've all done brilliantly." Kendrick was interested to discover that the commendation wasn't costing him, and that he could even build on it. "We could never have got to the extraordinary truth of it all without you. And on a personal level I'm very grateful." This time the smile was rueful, and

Peter and Phyllida knew the DCS's gratitude included the removal of his wife's cousin from his back.

"It's such a strange business," Peter said. "The publicity will be enormous."

"It's already started. I'm holding a press conference in" – Kendrick consulted his watch – "half an hour's time."

"No publicity for us," Steve said wistfully.

"Count yourselves lucky, if unfairly without praise."

"How will you explain your discoveries?" Peter asked with interest.

"We shan't. 'From information received' will have to cover it. The media will be getting so much else, we're unlikely to be pressed on it, if you'll excuse the pun. And it won't leak out" – stern for the only time since they had sat down, Kendrick swept a dark gaze across the three of them, eliciting three reflex nods – "because the only people who know apart from yourselves are the few members of my staff I recruited to carry out the raid and they were briefed beforehand on the need for absolute secrecy." Kendrick leaned back, his face relenting, and as his visitors made the moves of departure he picked up the coffee-pot and told them there was time for another cup.

★　★　★

"One thing I *can* do this time," Phyllida said, when she and Peter were back at the Agency, and in their usual positions on each side of his desk. "I can go back to the scene of the crime as myself to visit Mrs Anderson, and maybe take her out. Nothing different apart from my marital status, and what's a Mrs or a Miss between friends?" And nothing else personal to worry about, now there was no chance of seeing Dr Clifford.

"I should say you'll have to do it quickly. With all the senior staff removed, and no one at the back to bring on replacements, I don't see how the place can keep going."

"You're right. May I go this afternoon? I'll ring Kendrick and explain why I'll be there, so that if he's there too, or any of his men in the know, they won't shoot me. I'll be able to offer a bit of comfort to Debbie, as well."

"Of course you may go. There's nothing I want from you today. Or for the rest of the week."

"I've got one of my own clients coming in tomorrow morning. I don't want to take any time off work, Peter."

"What about Edinburgh?"

"What do you mean?"

"It's important, isn't it?"

She stared at him. "It could be. But you said ... you said you knew it wasn't."

"That was to provoke you into contradicting me," Peter said apologetically. "I should know you better."

"You know me well enough if you know Edinburgh's important. You can tell the time without looking at a clock or a watch, but how do you know *that*?"

"Oh, just the way you looked when you talked about going. Once when you mentioned it you looked furtive. Another time you had a little private smile."

"Oh, dear."

"If you go, will you come back?"

"Oh, Peter, why am I thinking of going at all? When I'm already happier than I've ever been in my life!"

"You are? I can't believe it!"

"It's true."

"Then it's wonderful." But the expressive face was suddenly glum. "Love's tough. It cuts through everything."

She didn't deny the application of his adage to herself, and saw the remains of hope die out of his eyes.

"You're so bloody blessed, Phyllida," he said at last.

"I've never thought so. Quite the reverse. But I'm blessed now to be working with you. And to be your friend as well as your colleague."

"We'll always be friends." But in a moment of shocked revelation, Peter found himself wondering if friendship was all he felt for his second-in-command. "I was thinking of a partnership," he rallied truthfully. "Business, I mean." He made himself smile at the absurdity of its being thought to mean anything else.

"Oh, Peter."

"You'd better go to Edinburgh," he said. "Things won't be the same – here – if you don't. And if you come back they'll be better than ever, as Piper and Moon."

"All right." He had made her decision for her, and she was grateful. As for so much else.

"Say next week?"

"Yes. Thank you."

He reached down beside his desk, brought up the bottles and the glasses. "We've never done this before in daylight, but there's a first time for everything." Peter stilled his busy hands as their eyes met and expressionlessly held.

"Dear Peter," Phyllida said.

"Dear Phyllida. Now, go and invite Jenny to join us: there are other kinds of drinks down here. And Steve if he's still around. Solving the case of the empty-headed corpse is something to celebrate."